Penguin
Speculative
Fiction
Special

This Penguin Speculative Fiction Special is part of a hardcover series of horror, science fiction, fantasy, and more published by Penguin Classics. Featuring custom endpapers, specially commissioned cover art, and introductions by scholars and notable figures, these collectible editions celebrate classics that invite us to ask, 'What if?' and that, through bold imagination, alternative visions, and magical realms, transform our perception of our world.

The first vampire short story in English, *The Vampyre* by John Polidori, and the first vampire novella, *Carmilla* by Sheridan Le Fanu, are published together in one volume. *The Vampyre*, first published in 1819 as both a short story and in book form, features Lord Ruthven, a deathly pale yet fatally charismatic nobleman who preys on women of high society; it is generally considered the first fully developed vampire narrative in English literature. *The Vampyre* is here accompanied by Alaric Watts's introduction, with which it was published throughout the nineteenth century, and which contains important supplementary material on vampire beliefs. *Carmilla* (1871–2) by Sheridan Le Fanu is a Gothic novella featuring a protagonist who typifies the long line of female and lesbian vampires in literature, movies, television series, and art. In a castle deep in the Austrian forest, Laura, a young woman, leads an isolated life with her father. A horse-drawn carriage crashes and an unexpected guest, the mysterious and seductive Carmilla, enters their lives. An early, sophisticated, and influential vampire novel, *Carmilla* predates Bram Stoker's *Dracula* by twenty-five years and the original *Nosferatu* film by fifty.

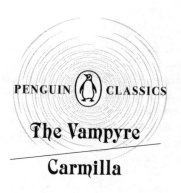

PENGUIN CLASSICS

The Vampyre
Carmilla

JOHN POLIDORI (1795–1821) was born in London to an Italian im-
migrant father and English mother. He studied medicine at the University of Edinburgh, graduated at the age of just nineteen, and in
1816 became physician to Lord Byron. He accompanied Byron on a
tour through Europe, famously spending the summer at the Villa
Diodati in Switzerland where they regularly met with the poet Percy
Bysshe Shelley, his partner Mary Godwin (later Shelley), and her
half-sister Claire Clairmont. It was here that Mary Shelley's novel
Frankenstein was inspired, influenced in part—as recorded in Polidori's diary—by Polidori's conversation and behaviour. Although
Polidori's fractious relationship with Byron led them to part ways,
they remained on cordial terms until the publication of Polidori's
tale *The Vampyre* in 1819, which was willfully misattributed to
Byron by the publisher Henry Colburn. Polidori was attempting to
realise his literary ambitions by publishing *The Vampyre*, extracts
from his diary, a volume of drama and poetry, and a novel he began
at Diodati (*Ernestus Berchtold; or, The Modern Œdipus*). However,
the controversy surrounding *The Vampyre* sank his writing career
and he published little else. He died by his own hand in 1821.

(JOSEPH THOMAS) SHERIDAN LE FANU (1814–1873) was born in Dublin to staunch Protestant parents descended from French Huguenots.
He studied law at Trinity College Dublin, and while he maintained
a somewhat desultory legal practice after graduating, his chief energies were directed towards fiction and journalism. He published his
first novel, the historical adventure *The Cock and Anchor*, in 1845,
and edited several newspapers during his lifetime—notably the *Dublin University Magazine*, in which he serialised his own stories and,

despite his Irish nationalist Tory sympathies, took a relaxed editorial line. Le Fanu found his distinctive authorial voice in mysteries and thrillers such as *The House by the Church-Yard* (1861–3), *Wylder's Hand* (1863–4), and *Uncle Silas* (1864), and in his collections of uncanny and supernatural tales—most famously *In a Glass Darkly* (1872)—which are often haunted by Irish politics and history. Known as 'The Invisible Prince' in Dublin due to his solitary and nocturnal lifestyle, Le Fanu died a recluse in 1873.

VICTORIA 'V. E.' SCHWAB is the #1 *New York Times* bestselling author of more than twenty books, including the acclaimed Shades of Magic universe, the Villains series, the City of Ghosts series, *Gallant*, *The Invisible Life of Addie LaRue*, and *The Fragile Threads of Power*. When not haunting Paris streets or trudging up English hillsides, she lives in Edinburgh, Scotland, and is usually tucked in the corner of a coffee shop, dreaming up monsters.

NICK GROOM is Professor of Literature in English at the University of Macau, having previously held positions at the universities of Bristol, Stanford, Chicago, and Exeter—at the last of which he is an honorary professor. He has published widely in literary criticism and cultural history, and among his recent books are *The Seasons: A Celebration of the English Year* (2014) and *Tolkien in the Twenty-First Century: The Meaning of Middle-Earth Today* (2023), both of which were shortlisted for literary prizes. He is best known for his work on the Gothic, which includes editions of several major Gothic novels (*The Castle of Otranto*, *The Italian*, *The Monk*, and *Frankenstein*), his study *The Vampire: A New History* (2020), and *The Gothic: A Very Short Introduction* (2012)—a standard work in the field that has earnt him the sobriquet 'The Prof. of Goth' from the experimental 'dark folk' musician Jordan Reyne. He lives on the Pearl River Delta in Macau, and on Dartmoor in Devon, England.

JOHN POLIDORI

The Vampyre

SHERIDAN LE FANU

Carmilla

Foreword by V. E. SCHWAB

Edited with an Introduction and Notes by NICK GROOM

PENGUIN BOOKS

PENGUIN BOOKS

An imprint of Penguin Random House LLC
1745 Broadway, New York, NY 10019
penguinrandomhouse.com

Foreword © 2025 by V. E. Schwab
Introduction, note on the text, notes, and suggestions for further reading
copyright © 2025 by Nick Groom

Set in Sabon LT Pro
Designed by Sabrina Bowers

LIBRARY OF CONGRESS CATALOGING-IN-PUBLICATION DATA
ISBN 9780143139003 (hardcover)
ISBN 9780593513132 (ebook)

Printed in the United States of America
1st Printing

The authorized representative in the EU for product safety and compliance
is Penguin Random House Ireland, Morrison Chambers, 32 Nassau Street,
Dublin D02 YH68, Ireland, https://eu-contact.penguin.ie.

Contents

Foreword

We rarely encounter monsters that lure us in as strongly as they frighten us away.

Beings that play on desire as well as fear, trapping their victims and readers between the two extremes. And vampires *are* creatures of extremes. They are pendulums, forever swinging capriciously between the opposites of romance and horror, love and violence, promise and peril.

They contain contradictory aspects, and those contradictions take root in us and flourish. Their very existence engenders both confusion and curiosity, forces that seem to draw us closer, even as instinct tells us to retreat.

They are by turns beautiful and horrifying, seductive and repulsive. They oscillate between stranger and friend, ally and foe. They exist between life and death, largely immune to the toil of either. Simultaneously suspended in time and outside of it.

They are mysterious to the point of being unknowable, which fills the mortals in their midst with dread.

And at the same time, they represent the directional course of knowledge itself.

The door that only swings one way.

The fact that what is known can never be unknown again.

They are experience incarnate, come to rend naïveté as easily as flesh. To strip away the trappings of innocence, of ignorance, of virtue, and expose the dark that runs in all of us. Waiting to be bled.

They are exposure, which can either be interpreted as corruption or enlightenment, and once the veil's been lifted, the door's been open, the threshold crossed, there is no going back.

(Even if it kills us.)

They hunger, and so they feed.

They want, and so they take.

They are forbidden, because they do not play by the rules—of society, of nature, of man. The same rules that insist on a binary of good and evil, moral and depraved. The vampires' pendulous swing denies that binary, and instead presents a spectrum. Lines blurring, black and white giving way to gray.

Perhaps that is yet one more reason they've persisted when so many other monsters have fallen out of literary favour.

Despite their archetypal trappings—the fangs, the thirst, the coffin, the cape—vampires are surprisingly malleable characters, able to change with (or more accurately, *adapt* so that they stand in opposition to) the times in which they're written.

The rules that bind them shift depending on the century, the storyteller.

Sometimes they are so tethered to the dark that the merest sunlight burns them. Sometimes they are so reviled by heaven that they cannot set foot in a church or touch a holy relic. So impure that they cannot handle silver. So of the dead that they must sleep beneath the earth. Sometimes they are monstrous, visibly inhuman.

Other times, they blend in so well that they could almost pass for one of us (though some small sliver always gives them away:

their manner, their charm, some glint of the supernatural, or the barest hint of fang).

But regardless of what shape they take—whether it's a new lover, or a bloodstained fiend; a bosom friend, or an animal stalking its next meal—regardless of whether they smile warmly or show us their teeth, we are unfailingly drawn to them. Across stories. Across centuries.

Because in addition to sex and death, there is something else the vampire has always—and will always—represent, whether or not the author sanctions it.

Permission.

Permission to take pleasure, in sex, in life, in everything.

Permission to defy the roles and rules set out by society.

Permission to break free of expectations.

Permission to crave. To hunger.

To want.

And just like the vampire that inspires it, want—genuine want—has the power to simultaneously terrify and thrill us. And so, when faced with either—with both—we are torn between the urge to recoil and rush into its arms.

To accept the embrace.

And the cost.

There is a cost, of course, for giving in to that desire. In these stories, it is a price paid with blood, with innocence, with life. An old self, shed in the making of the new one. A violent transaction, and a reminder that vampire tales might present themselves as romance, but they were born from horror.

No wonder so many find themselves halting at that final threshold, shrinking back into the safety of their well-lit rooms, instead of following the monsters—and their hearts—into the dark.

V. E. SCHWAB

Introduction

Vampires—as opposed to bloodsucking monsters in general—
have been a recognized part of Western culture only since the
early eighteenth century. They were first named and described
in news items across Europe in 1732, following medical cases
of purported outbreaks of vampirism in Eastern Europe that
had been reported to the authorities in Vienna, capital of the
Habsburg Empire. Investigating officials described how the dead
were apparently rising after weeks of internment in the grave,
before attacking family and friends—either strangling them or
infecting them with disease; they also often drank the blood of
their victims. Military surgeons conducted exhumations and au-
topsies of vampire corpses, and carefully recorded forensic
details—the bodies were found to be fresh, while their coffins
were awash with blood; victims, meanwhile, exhibited a variety
of physical and psychological symptoms, including bruises around
the neck and dreadful nightmares. Witnesses and relatives were
interviewed and testified before magistrates to the veracity of these
vampire attacks, while suspected vampires were dispatched in a
variety of arcane ways—most commonly by staking, decapitation, or cremation. This corporeality was what distinguished
vampires from other manifestations of the undead, such as ghosts:

Vampires were tangible beings that needed to feed, but could be slain by physical means.

For several years in the middle of the eighteenth century, then, there appeared to be an unearthly epidemic of vampirism. This pestilential phenomenon gripped the attention of pathologists, theologians, and philosophers—dramatizing, in effect, the confrontation of Enlightenment thinking with Eastern European folklore. Vampires were linked to the 'incubus', a suffocating demon that brought nightmares, as well as to the Eastern Orthodox Church. The Orthodox Church had split from Roman Catholicism in the eleventh century and consequently had, in some areas—such as the incorruptibility of corpses—developed different beliefs. For Catholics, an undecayed corpse was saintly; for Orthodox Christians, it was a sign of excommunication—so the fresh corpse of a vampire threatened Catholic convictions and subsequently led to a series of studies and publications, most notably the work of the popular Benedictine theologian Abbot Dom Augustin Calmet. Calmet's rational Catholic treatise *Dissertations upon the Apparitions of Angels, Dæmons, and Ghosts, and Concerning the Vampires of Hungary, Bohemia, Moravia, and Silesia* was first published in France before being translated into English in 1759 and republished in 1850; it became a manual and sourcebook of vampire lore. At the same time, vampires attracted the attention of the French *philosophes* Denis Diderot, Jean-Jacques Rousseau, and Voltaire as supposed cases of vampirism—attested as they were by eyewitnesses and endorsed by notaries—questioned the credibility and dependability of firsthand testimony and evidence.

Vampires were further researched by epidemiologists, as they were frequently associated with the virulent spread of contagious diseases and also prompted rather more mundane inquiries into areas such as whether the chemical composition of local soil could affect the decomposition of corpses, as well as the effects of regional diet on mental health. But the wider ethnography of communities living on the borders of the Habsburg Empire was a significant issue: these peripheral territories had originally been Ottoman possessions but were claimed by Vienna at the Treaty of Passarowitz in 1718 and so were now forcibly occupied by a new foreign power. The mass trauma experienced by these peoples may well have manifested itself as a belief in vampires, in which the absolute states of life and death were disturbed by the arrival of a new category: the undead.

Such speculation meant that publications poured from the press—vampires were, in the words of one critic, a 'media sensation'—but they also immediately became part of the common currency of social debate, political discourse, and satirical attacks.[1] From their first appearance in Britain, vampires were recognized as compelling images of corruption and consumption. Just as earlier bloodsuckers such as leeches had been alluded to in exposing the abuse of power and the exploitation of the vulnerable, the figure of the vampire was immediately understood as a potential metaphor in denouncing the ruling classes, and its origins—in peasant superstitions 1,500 miles away—were forgotten. 'Caleb D'Anvers', the earliest named commentator on vampires in Britain, claimed that the ruling classes of British society had been crawling with vampires for centuries, naming the royal favourite Piers Gaveston (d.1312) as the prototypical aristocratic parasite, before listing various other iniquitous noblemen and claiming that there were 'an Hundred more' of the same rank.[2] As such, for the rest of the century vampires were used in condemning avaricious merchants, larcenous investors, duplicitous dealers in stocks and shares, despicable slave traders, lying politicians and bureaucrats, rapacious landlords, heartless tax and debt collectors, and merciless lawyers, as well as immoral military officers and depraved clergymen, and, in the literary world, thieving plagiarists and mendacious critics.

This is the legacy of vampire literature that was bequeathed to Dr. John William Polidori for his short prose narrative *The Vampyre*, published in 1819, and to Joseph Sheridan Le Fanu for his novella *Carmilla*, published in 1871–2. Both tales draw heavily on eighteenth-century British representations of the vampire, while at the same time developing new aspects of a figure that would eventually culminate in Bram Stoker's *Dracula* (1897) before being tirelessly reinvented in multiple new ways and new media in the twentieth and twenty-first centuries.

THE VAMPYRE

The Vampyre and its Introduction were first published in April 1819, both in *The New Monthly Magazine* and simultaneously as a book; the texts were accompanied in the magazine by a 'Letter from Geneva, with Anecdotes of Lord Byron' derived from Polidori's diary, and by both the same letter and a spurious travelogue in the separate book publication. The work immediately provoked a ferocious row because in *The New Monthly The Vampyre* was blatantly attributed to Lord Byron; hence Byron and his allies instantly took furious—if understandable—offence. But this deception itself masked another subterfuge concerning the composition of the tale: the story of how *The Vampyre* came to be published is worth outlining not only because it is one of the most celebrated literary anecdotes of the period, but also because it has been significantly misrepresented—a misrepresentation that seriously affects the interpretation of the tale.

In April 1816, three years before the appearance in print of
The Vampyre, Byron had left England accompanied by his servants and his physician Dr. Polidori, travelling to the Villa Diodati on the banks of Lake Geneva in Switzerland. There they
met the poet Percy Bysshe Shelley, his paramour Mary Godwin
(who would become Mary Shelley at the end of the year), their
baby son William, and Mary's half-sister Claire Clairmont, preg-
nant with Byron's child. During their stay, Byron suggested that
they all write ghost stories—a challenge that allegedly inspired
both Mary Shelley's *Frankenstein*, published in 1818, and *The
Vampyre*. However, things are not so straightforward. Polidori,
who began his novel *Ernestus Berchtold* in response to Byron's parlour game, claimed that he wrote *The Vampyre* after
completing Byron's own abandoned ghost story—a half-written
vampire narrative that Byron had finished recounting one evening at the fireside. Polidori claimed to have finished the tale for
the amusement of a society lady, then left his manuscript in Geneva; two years later it mysteriously arrived at the offices of *The
New Monthly*. It was subsequently published, without permission
and under Byron's name.

This account, given by Polidori but inconsistently maintained, is almost certainly a fabrication and an attempt to distance himself from the venture. It transpires that Polidori himself
not only delivered *The Vampyre* to *The New Monthly*, but probably wrote it as late as March 1819 in a deal struck with Henry
Colburn, the magazine's publisher, to print the *Vampyre* papers
as a taster for his novel *Ernestus Berchtold*, published later in
the year. Colburn was not simply eager to capitalize on Byron's
fame and notoriety, but may well have seen an opportunity to
respond to Johann Wolfgang von Goethe's 'The Bride of Corinth',
a vampire poem inspired by the myths of ancient Greece that
had appeared in *Blackwood's Magazine* the previous month.

Polidori was in the process of brokering a deal for his novel with Colburn and possessed an unpublished diary full of tidbits about his travels with Byron in 1816, and so had surely mentioned Byron's fragmentary vampire tale. The only manuscript was with Byron, and Polidori evidently remembered very little after two and a half years—not even the name of the protagonist—but he recalled enough of the overall plot to write out his own version. Even so, he was very careful to emphasize that the original idea was Byron's: if *The Vampyre* was to be published, Polidori stressed that it be published with a disclaimer stating that the original idea at the Villa Diodati was Byron's—a note that Colburn simply cut on the eve of publication, falsely attributing the whole tale to Byron.

Alaric Watts, sub-editor on *The New Monthly*, subsequently confirmed this version of events in letters to and meetings with Byron's circle; he also stated that Polidori had been paid—thus confirming Polidori's close involvement with the project. Watts wrote the Introduction to *The Vampyre* and reworked the tale into a publishable state, and arguably also proposed the name of the protagonist. Seeing Colburn's dishonest revision of authorship on publication, Watts promptly resigned; Polidori, meanwhile, battled on, attempting in a series of letters to the press to explain and justify his actions and save his honour as a gentleman and reputation as a writer—both without success.

It is difficult, then, to separate *The Vampyre* from Polidori's misleading and unreliable account of its composition and publication as he—perhaps more than any of those present—sought to canonize the Diodati summer and place himself at the heart of Gothic Romanticism. Indeed, a spurious third canto of *Don Juan*, published on 15 July 1819—within four days of Byron's first two cantos appearing, and just two and a half months after the publication of *The Vampyre*—shows that this writerly

summit had already been memorialized as the most infamous
literary episode of the day:

> In rival conclave there and dark divan
>   He met and mingled with the Vampyre crew
> Who hate the virtues and the form of man,
>   And strive to bring fresh monsters into view;
> Who mock the inscrutable Almighty's plan
>   By seeking truth and order to subdue—
> Scribblers, who fright the novel reading train
> With mad creations of th' unsettled brain.
>
> There Frankenstein was hatched—the wretch abhorred,
>   Whom shuddering Sh——y [Shelley] saw in horrid dream
> Plying his task where human bones are stored,
>   And there the Vampyre quaffed the living stream
> From beauty's veins—such sights could joy afford,
>   To this strange coterie, glorying in each theme,
> That wakes disgust in other minds—LORD HAROLD
> Sung wildly too, but none knew what he carolled.[3]

However, disentangling *The Vampyre* from Polidori's lies re-
stores the chronology of literary history, as it can be seen that
The Vampyre was certainly written *after* Mary Shelley's *Frankenstein* and is indeed indebted to it. Aubrey shares many characteristics with Victor Frankenstein: he suffers a comparable
breakdown and even wanders the streets at night. Lord Ruthven, in contrast, has all the strength and cunning of the Being,
and likewise predates on innocent women—hanging over their
corpses like a nightmare. Moreover, even minor details such as
the agency of moonlight, the swearing of fatal oaths, and the
triggering effects of a miniature painting are repeated. Reading

The Vampyre as a post-*Frankenstein* text shows how Polidori, an insider at the Villa Diodati, was reminded in reading *Frankenstein* of the tensions and intimacies of that summer and revived this atmosphere of passion and threat in his own Chamber work.

Polidori's tale begins in London with the arrival of the mysterious and uncanny Lord Ruthven (pronounced *riven*), before describing his travels across the Continent and into Turkey with his young and naïve companion, Aubrey. As Ruthven moves imperiously from scandal to scandal, leaving degradation and despair in his wake, Aubrey, in contrast, falls in love and leaves his sinister companion. It is at this point, in Greece, that Aubrey learns of the existence of vampires. Yet these vampires—which are only ever hinted at—are not the Eastern European undead killers detailed by Watts in his Introduction to the tale, but derive from Eastern Mediterranean superstitions. Watts does indeed begin his Introduction by stating that vampires originated in the East—by which he means the Middle East—and quotes from Byron's Turkish narrative poem *The Giaour* (1813) at length; nevertheless he then focuses on the Habsburg reports. Polidori, in contrast, mixes Greek and Turkish vampire lore more explicitly into his conception of the figure, drawing on Robert Southey's Islamic epic poem *Thalaba the Destroyer* (1801) and Byron's *The Giaour*—as well as on Goethe's 'The Bride of Corinth'—rather than on the Habsburg accounts. Consequently, *The Vampyre* combines Hellenic and Islamic sources in a contemporary social setting, and, as had been the case in depictions of the vampire over the previous eighty-plus years, Polidori maintained the status of the figure as an aristocrat—and a British aristocrat to boot—free to roam across fashionable Europe.

While the travels of Ruthven and Aubrey clearly reflect Polidori's experience of riding to Switzerland in Byron's luxurious carriage and socializing with him there, it would be wrong simply to equate Ruthven and Aubrey with Byron and Polidori, respectively. As he did with the memories evoked by *Frankenstein*, Polidori reworks and complicates his material. The relationship between Ruthven and Aubrey is deeply ambiguous and entangled in unspoken desires, and a careful reader will perceive not only hints of homoeroticism and narcissism between the two, but also a potential exchange of identities. Aubrey develops as many vampiric characteristics of his own as those he perceives in Ruthven, before descending into delusion and madness. If Polidori is dramatizing himself as Aubrey, he is—strangely— doing so as an outsider documenting his own psychic breakdown. Likewise, while Ruthven's fatal erotic charisma may certainly suggest Byron's sexual appetites, seductive vampires were in any case nothing new and had already featured in several poems. More importantly, though, Ruthven lacks Byron's personal characteristics: his affability, his 'excessive' vanity, his 'extreme' irritability. Henry Southern remembered that Byron was 'capricious, full of humours, apt to be offended, and wilful'; he also chewed tobacco.[4] Ruthven is quite different—and not really a portrait of Byron at all. Neither is Ruthven an alienated 'Byronic' anti-hero—the tale is far more subtle and ambiguous than that. Polidori is really using the word *vampire* more figuratively: for a 'malignant and loathsome character . . . who preys ruthlessly upon others'.[5]

So is Ruthven even a vampire? Aubrey is a delusional character at the nightmarish centre of his own vampiric delirium, and readers should consider the extent to which the entire affair could be a protracted nightmare.[6] Six months after *The Vampyre* had been published, an article in the *Imperial Magazine* discussed Polidori's tale in such hallucinatory terms:

The Vampyre is represented as a mere creature of the imagination; to which have been ascribed fictitious powers, corresponding, in their application, with those which we attribute to sylphs, fairies, elves, and genii. The superstructure, built upon this imaginary basis, coincides, in its visionary materials, with the foundation on which it rests. The dark and gloomy thoughts thus embodied, seem admirably adapted to keep alive the fiction. . . . Under its imposing aspect, the mind of the reader is insensibly transported into a region of enchantment. . . . Awakened from this poetic delirium, when we reach the conclusion of the tale, reason once more regains its dominion over fancy; but, unfortunately, instead of following that steady light, which is necessary to all just discrimination, we suddenly fall into an opposite snare, and hastily conclude that the Vampyre has no kind of existence, except in the dreams of poets, and the fables of romance.[7]

What kind of existence does the vampire really have?

While the literary debate surrounding *The Vampyre* rolled on, within a year the tale had been adapted for the stage, proving a runaway success in a variety of productions, from operas, burlesques, ballets, and farces to a state-of-the-art, special-effect-laden spectacular set in the Celtic mysticism of Ossianic Scotland in which Ruthven vanished before the eyes of the startled audience. As the actor-manager John Coleman later remembered:

Oh, goroo! When I recall that gruesome Scottish horror feeding upon the blood of young maidens and throwing himself headlong through the solid stage, and vanishing into the regions below amidst flames of red fire, I protest I shudder at it now.[8]

Indeed, by November 1819 *The New Monthly* could report that:

SINCE the appearance of the story of the *Vampire*, the conversation of private parties has frequently turned on the subject; and the discussion has been prolonged and invigorated by the pieces brought out at the theatres, as well of Paris as of London. Vampirism, at one period, had almost superseded politics, at Paris, in the journals. . . . This article deserves attention, no less from its temporary interest, than from its peculiar character, as part of the history of the human mind.[9]

What John Polidori and Alaric Watts achieved with *The Vampyre*, then, was in part to establish various characteristics for later portrayals of vampires—the persistent gaze, the ashen complexion, their magnetic attraction—but the most enduring innovation was to make the vampire an independent individual, an autonomous character. Indeed, a contemporary review of *The Vampyre* complained that 'the author of this tale has made the vampyre-hero of it a bustling inhabitant of the world; restless and erratic; a nobleman subject to disappointments,—to pecuniary embarrassments, . . . —and even to death'.[10] Readings of *The Vampyre* tend to be overshadowed or distorted either by the credulous acceptance that it was composed at the Villa Diodati in 1816 or by uncritical assertions that it is a character assassination of Lord Byron. Yet the very features that this reviewer condemns are what would turn the vampire into an iconic figure: nearly seventy years later, Count Dracula—international import/export specialist and investor in real estate—is himself a 'bustling inhabitant of the world'. *The Vampyre* has deservedly become a touchstone of Gothic fiction as the first English vampire tale in prose, and an uncomfortable archetype of the vampire character—yet all of this was to be cold comfort to Polidori: two years after publication he died by his own hand.[11]

CARMILLA

Turning to Joseph Sheridan Le Fanu's *Carmilla* (1871–2) after *The Vampyre* confronts us with a very different entity. Yes, *Carmilla* is explicitly indebted to eighteenth-century vampirology, and the two texts have many features in common: picturesque landscapes and a sense of the deep past and the recovery of history—Hellenic archaeology in *The Vampyre*, the ruins of Castle Karnstein in *Carmilla*; the ambiguous identities and altered mental states of Aubrey and Laura—'I don't know myself' murmurs Laura at one point (p. 62); the mysterious agency of the moon; and the worlds of aristocratic wealth, society balls, and even cross-dressing masquerades. Both texts also withhold the nature of vampirism, which, especially in *Carmilla*, remains opaque until the end of the tale. Furthermore, the plots of both *The Vampyre* and *Carmilla* turn on paintings: the miniature of Lord Marsden in *The Vampyre*, the portrait of Mircalla in *Carmilla*. Like other Gothic literature of the period, from Edgar Allan Poe's 'The Oval Portrait' (1842) to Oscar Wilde's *The Picture of Dorian Gray* (1890)—as well as several other vampire tales—*The Vampyre* and *Carmilla* are characterized by ekphrasis. But all this misses the sheer power of *Carmilla*: it is a tour de force of female sensuality.

The plot of *Carmilla* describes the encounter between Laura, an English girl living in Styria (one of the Habsburg territories), and the mysterious Carmilla, who is suddenly plunged into Laura's world and is invited to stay by her father. Laura has already met Carmilla in an eerie childhood dream that begins the tale, and they then discover they are blood relations through Laura's mother, now dead; Carmilla also has some connection with the region and the nearby ruined castle.

Carmilla herself is not only wildly alluring—'certainly the

most beautiful creature I had ever seen' (p. 58)—but insistently sexual and intensely passionate; yet at the same time she inspires distaste, disgust, repugnance. Laura is both besotted and sickened by her adoring gaze, her hot kisses, her ardent possessiveness—she trembles in ecstasy and shudders in revulsion. For Carmilla, Laura is her 'Darling, darling'; she enters Laura's body—'I live in you' (p. 74)—and commands her thoughts and emotions. In part, Laura's responses are a confused knot of stifling claustrophobia—the high emotions of sexual awakening and unspoken lesbian desire—but they go deeper too: Carmilla replaces Laura's absent mother to guide the daughter into womanhood, yet at the same time is vulnerable, infantile, and feeds from the younger girl.

Laura is lovesick for her companion who teases and arouses, manipulates and torments her—literally lovesick, for Carmilla is a vector of contagion and the text is 'a narrative of infection'.[12] Not only is the physical and hallucinatory listlessness of the lovers feverish, but their community is in the grip of an inexplicable and fatal epidemic, and is also infested with superstition and terror. In this, the tale deliberately draws on the eighteenth-century belief that vampires were active spreaders of disease; moreover, the symptoms of illness were also recognisable from these earlier historical reports—notably as the incubus of nightmare asphyxiating its victim, but also including preventative measures taken against contracting malaria. Le Fanu accordingly cites specific works of eighteenth-century vampirology, firmly placing the work in the context of the previous century with an emphasis on medical diagnosis, forensic evidence, witness testimony, military investigation, and legal deposition. Furthermore, the tale is presented as the case notes of one 'Doctor Hesselius', edited for publication by his assistant and yet written in the first person—through which it incorporates

textual games in citing barely credible letters and unreliable nar-
rators, and includes a story-within-a-story and even linguistic
puzzles. So while it is perhaps tempting to speculate about the
relationship between, say, vampirism, menstruation, and virgin-
ity, the detail of the vampire's coffin floating with blood—'in
which to a depth of seven inches, the body lay immersed' (p.
134)—is directly derived from these earlier eighteenth-century
reports.

The Styrian setting and the eighteenth-century vampire lore
of *Carmilla* have also encouraged critics to read the text as a
commentary on Eastern European politics, although one scholar
admits that 'There is little surviving documentary evidence that
J. S. Le Fanu showed any enthusiasm for the Eastern Question'.[13]
More convincingly, perhaps—and given Le Fanu's family back-
ground as the son of a Protestant minister who was born and
worked in Dublin—the tale has instead been considered in the
context of Anglo-Irish politics. Laura's position as a trans-
planted English girl living close by ancient ruins may reflect the
marginalized Protestant Ascendancy in nineteenth-century Ireland uncomfortably cohabiting with the remains of the old Roman
Catholic order and observing the rise of a new, upwardly mobile
Catholic middle class. Anglo-Irish politics had indeed long been
represented in vampiric terms, yet despite the origins of the Gothic
in English Protestantism and Whig politics—and notwithstanding the continued anti-Catholic stance of much nineteenth-
century Gothic literature—*Carmilla* should not be simplistically
reduced to 'Catholic magic'.[14] Le Fanu was acutely aware of the
distinctive facets of eighteenth-century vampirology and its
roots in Eastern European and Orthodox superstition, the theories of Enlightenment science and medicine, and the ensuing de-
bates concerning verification and testimony. What Le Fanu
succeeds in doing, then, is to combine the dramatic, plot-driven

verve of Polidori's *The Vampyre* with the rational inquiries of medical, legal, and legislative authority to create a vampire tale that calmly references the reports and research of the previous century. At the same time, he presents this through a psychologically sophisticated relationship of same-sex female desire. Female vampires may have been common in this period, but are seldom as carnal as in this tale; nonetheless, *Carmilla* portrays an unnervingly contemporary account of the devastating seduction of a young girl by a beautiful she-vampire of labyrinthine psychological intricacy and intoxicating hunger.

CONCLUSION

The Vampyre and *Carmilla* are, with the obvious exception of Bram Stoker's *Dracula*, the best-known and most widely read nineteenth-century vampire tales—and they were published at a time when vampire literature was as popular as it is today. Nineteenth-century vampires appeared in verse, in fiction, and on the stage; for British readers and audiences they could be English, Scottish, Irish, American, French, German, Austro-Hungarian, and African; likewise, they could be Protestant, Orthodox, Islamic, or Jewish; and they could be male or female, affluent or indigent, exquisite or monstrous, heterosexual or homosexual, metamorphic or invisible, and murderous, tragic, or comic.[15] The one thing that nineteenth-century vampires could not be is homogenous: they are as different—and as balefully bewitching—as are the vampires of John William Polidori and Joseph Sheridan Le Fanu themselves.

NICK GROOM

A Note on the Text

There are two printings of *The Vampyre*. It was first published on 1 April 1819 in *The New Monthly Magazine*, and then separately published as a book printed in the same week. The text was clearly reset for the book, and as this is the basis for the version that was most widely disseminated in the nineteenth century, it is from this setting that the current text is taken. In any case, differences are minor and are mainly issues of punctuation, while obvious typos such as 'lmost' and 'affliced' have been silently corrected. Likewise, triple dashes are replaced by an em-rule, and quadruple dashes by a double em-rule. Both texts were published with the Introduction by Alaric Watts, which was lightly revised for the book from the text of *The New Monthly*. Current editions sometimes omit the Introduction—an unfortunate shortcoming as it is a significant source of vampire lore in the century—or, if included, it is often unannotated (see D. L. Macdonald and Kathleen Scherf's otherwise excellent edition for the University of Toronto Press, 1994). Macdonald and Scherf edited *The Vampyre* from a copy of the book annotated by Polidori for an imagined second edition that was never published and so made striking changes—such as revising the name Ruthven to Strongmore—that were not available to readers until their edition was published.

Carmilla was first serialized in the journal *The Dark Blue* in 1871–2 before being published in Le Fanu's collection *In a Glass Darkly* (vol. 3) later in 1872. While the version in *In a Glass Darkly* contains only minor revisions, it also importantly adds a Prologue—so, once again, as this was the text most widely available to nineteenth-century readers, it is the version used here. The textual changes are recorded by Kathleen Costello-Sullivan in *Carmilla: A Critical Edition* (Syracuse University Press, 2013). Obvious errors, such as 'the' for 'they' and 'good-night' for 'good night', have been corrected, and capitalization of chapter titles and opening words has been ignored.

The Vampyre

JOHN POLIDORI

1819 Introduction

by Alaric Watts

The superstition upon which this tale is founded is very general in the East. Among the Arabians it appears to be common: it did not, however, extend itself to the Greeks until after the establishment of Christianity; and it has only assumed its present form since the division of the Latin and Greek churches;[1] at which time, the idea becoming prevalent, that a Latin body could not corrupt if buried in their territory, it gradually increased, and formed the subject of many wonderful stories, still extant, of the dead rising from their graves, and feeding upon the blood of the young and beautiful. In the West it spread, with some slight variation, all over Hungary, Poland, Austria, and Lorraine, where the belief existed, that vampyres nightly imbibed a certain portion of the blood of their victims, who became emaciated, lost their strength, and speedily died of consumptions; whilst these human blood-suckers fattened—and their veins became distended to such a state of repletion, as to cause the blood to flow from all the passages of their bodies, and even from the very pores of their skins.

In the London Journal, of March, 1732, is a curious, and, of course, *credible* account of a particular case of vampyrism, which is stated to have occurred at Madreyga, in Hungary. It appears, that upon an examination of the commander-in-chief and magistrates of the place, they positively and unanimously affirmed, that, about five years before, a certain Heyduke, named Arnold Paul,[2] had been heard to say, that, at Cassovia, on the frontiers of the Turkish Servia, he had been tormented by a vampyre, but had found a way to rid himself of the evil, by eating some of the earth out of the vampyre's grave, and rubbing himself with his blood. This precaution, however, did not prevent him from becoming a vampyre* himself; for, about twenty or thirty days after his death and burial, many persons complained of having been tormented by him, and a deposition was made, that four persons had been deprived of life by his attacks. To prevent further mischief, the inhabitants having consulted their Hadagni,† took up the body, and found it (as is supposed to be usual in cases of vampyrism) fresh, and entirely free from corruption, and emitting at the mouth, nose, and ears, pure and florid blood. Proof having been thus obtained, they resorted to the accustomed remedy. A stake was driven entirely through the heart and body of Arnold Paul, at which he is reported to have cried out as dreadfully as if he had been alive. This done, they cut off his head, burned his body, and threw the ashes into his grave. The same measures were adopted with the corses[3] of those persons who had previously died from vampyrism, lest they should, in their turn, become agents upon others who survived them.

This monstrous rodomontade is here related, because it seems

---

*The universal belief is, that a person sucked by a vampyre becomes a vampyre himself, and sucks in his turn. [Watts's note.]

†Chief bailiff. [Watts's note.]

better adapted to illustrate the subject of the present observations than any other instance which could be adduced. In many parts of Greece it is considered as a sort of punishment after death, for some heinous crime committed whilst in existence, that the deceased is not only doomed to vampyrise, but compelled to confine his infernal visitations solely to those beings he loved most while upon earth—those to whom he was bound by ties of kindred and affection.—A supposition alluded to in the 'Giaour.'

> But first on earth, as Vampyre sent,
> Thy corse shall from its tomb be rent;
> Then ghastly haunt the native place,
> And suck the blood of all thy race;
> There from thy *daughter, sister, wife,*
> At midnight drain the stream of life;
> *Yet loathe the banquet which perforce*
> Must feed thy livid living corse,
> Thy victims, ere they yet expire,
> Shall know the demon for their sire;
> As cursing thee, thou cursing them,
> Thy flowers are withered on the stem.
> But one that for *thy crime* must fall,
> The youngest, best beloved of all,
> Shall bless thee with a *father's* name—
> That word shall wrap thy heart in flame!
> Yet thou must end thy task and mark
> Her cheek's last tinge—her eye's last spark,
> And the last glassy glance must view
> Which freezes o'er its lifeless blue;
> Then with unhallowed hand shall tear
> The tresses of her yellow hair,

Of which, in life a lock when shorn
Affection's fondest pledge was worn—
But now is borne away by thee
Memorial of thine agony!
Yet with thine own best blood shall drip;
Thy gnashing tooth, and haggard lip;
Then stalking to thy sullen grave,
Go—and with Gouls and Afrits rave,
Till these in horror shrink away
From spectre more accursed than they.[4]

Mr. Southey has also introduced in his wild but beautiful poem of 'Thalaba,'[5] the vampyre corse of the Arabian maid Oneiza, who is represented as having returned from the grave for the purpose of tormenting him she best loved whilst in existence. But this cannot be supposed to have resulted from the sinfulness of her life, she being pourtrayed throughout the whole of the tale as a complete type of purity and innocence. The veracious Tournefort gives a long account in his travels of several astonishing cases of vampyrism, to which he pretends[6] to have been an eye-witness; and Calmet,[7] in his great work upon this subject, besides a variety of anecdotes, and traditionary narratives illustrative of its effects, has put forth some learned dissertations, tending to prove it to be a classical, as well as barbarian error.

Many curious and interesting notices on this singularly horrible superstition might be added; though the present may suffice for the limits of a note, necessarily devoted to explanation, and which may now be concluded by merely remarking, that though the term Vampyre is the one in most general acceptation, there are several others synonimous with it, which are made use of in various parts of the world: as Vroucolocha, Vardoulacha, Goul, Broucoloka, &c.

The Vampyre

It happened that in the midst of the dissipations attendant upon a London winter, there appeared at the various parties of the leaders of the *ton*[1] a nobleman, more remarkable for his singularities, than his rank. He gazed upon the mirth around him, as if he could not participate therein. Apparently, the light laughter of the fair only attracted his attention, that he might by a look quell it, and throw fear into those breasts where thoughtlessness reigned. Those who felt this sensation of awe, could not explain whence it arose: some attributed it to the dead grey eye, which, fixing upon the object's face, did not seem to penetrate, and at one glance to pierce through to the inward workings of the heart; but fell upon the cheek with a leaden ray that weighed upon the skin it could not pass. His peculiarities caused him to be invited to every house; all wished to see him, and those who had been accustomed to violent excitement, and now felt the weight of *ennui*,[2] were pleased at having something in their presence capable of engaging their attention. In spite of the deadly hue of his face, which never gained a warmer tint, either from the blush of modesty, or from the strong emotion of passion, though its form and outline were beautiful, many of the female hunters after notoriety attempted to win his attentions,

and gain, at least, some marks of what they might term affection: Lady Mercer,[3] who had been the mockery of every monster
shewn in drawing-rooms since her marriage, threw herself in his
way, and did all but put on the dress of a mountebank,[4] to attract his notice:—though in vain:—when she stood before him,
though his eyes were apparently fixed upon hers, still it seemed
as if they were unperceived;—even her unappalled impudence
was baffled, and she left the field. But though the common adultress could not influence even the guidance of his eyes, it was not
that the female sex was indifferent to him: yet such was the apparent caution with which he spoke to the virtuous wife and innocent daughter, that few knew he ever addressed himself to
females. He had, however, the reputation of a winning tongue;
and whether it was that it even overcame the dread of his singular character, or that they were moved by his apparent hatred of
vice, he was as often among those females who form the boast
of their sex from their domestic virtues, as among those who
sully it by their vices.

About the same time, there came to London a young gentleman of the name of Aubrey:[5] he was an orphan left with an only
sister in the possession of great wealth, by parents who died
while he was yet in childhood. Left also to himself by guardians, who thought it their duty merely to take care of his fortune, while they relinquished the more important charge of his
mind to the care of mercenary subalterns, he cultivated more his
imagination than his judgment. He had, hence, that high romantic feeling of honour and candour, which daily ruins so
many milliners' apprentices. He believed all to sympathise with
virtue, and thought that vice was thrown in by Providence
merely for the picturesque effect of the scene, as we see in ro-
mances: he thought that the misery of a cottage merely consisted
in the vesting of clothes, which were as warm, but which were

better adapted to the painter's eye[6] by their irregular folds and various coloured patches. He thought, in fine,[7] that the dreams of poets were the realities of life. He was handsome, frank, and rich: for these reasons, upon his entering into the gay[8] circles, many mothers surrounded him, striving which should describe with least truth their languishing or romping favourites: the daughters at the same time, by their brightening countenances when he approached, and by their sparkling eyes, when he opened his lips, soon led him into false notions of his talents and his merit. Attached as he was to the romance of his solitary hours, he was startled at finding, that, except in the tallow and wax candles that flickered, not from the presence of a ghost, but from want of snuffing, there was no foundation in real life for any of that congeries[9] of pleasing pictures and descriptions contained in those volumes, from which he had formed his study. Finding, however, some compensation in his gratified vanity, he was about to relinquish his dreams, when the extraordinary being we have above described, crossed him in his career.

He watched him; and the very impossibility of forming an idea of the character of a man entirely absorbed in himself, who gave few other signs of his observation of external objects, than the tacit assent to their existence, implied by the avoidance of their contact: allowing his imagination to picture every thing that flattered its propensity to extravagant ideas, he soon formed this object into the hero of a romance, and determined to observe the offspring of his fancy, rather than the person before him. He became acquainted with him, paid him attentions, and had so far advanced upon his notice, that his presence was always recognised. He gradually learnt that Lord Ruthven's[10] affairs were embarrassed, and soon found, from the notes of preparation in —— Street, that he was about to travel. Desirous of gaining some information respecting this singular character, who, till now, had only whetted his curiosity, he hinted to his guardians, that it was time for him to perform the tour, which for many generations has been thought necessary to enable the young to take some rapid steps in the career of vice towards putting themselves upon an equality with the aged, and not allowing them to appear as if fallen from the skies, whenever scandalous intrigues are mentioned as the subjects of pleasantry or of praise, according to the degree of skill shewn in carrying them on. They consented: and Aubrey immediately mentioning his intentions to Lord Ruthven, was surprised to receive from him a proposal to join him. Flattered by such a mark of esteem from him, who, apparently, had nothing in common with other men, he gladly accepted it, and in a few days they had passed the circling waters.[11]

Hitherto, Aubrey had had no opportunity of studying Lord Ruthven's character, and now he found, that, though many more of his actions were exposed to his view, the results offered different conclusions from the apparent motives to his conduct. His companion was profuse in his liberality;—the idle, the vagabond, and the beggar, received from his hand more than enough to relieve their immediate wants. But Aubrey could not avoid remarking, that it was not upon the virtuous, reduced to indigence by the misfortunes attendant even upon virtue, that he bestowed his alms;—these were sent from the door with hardly suppressed sneers; but when the profligate came to ask something, not to relieve his wants, but to allow him to wallow in his lust, or to sink him still deeper in his iniquity, he was sent away with rich charity. This was, however, attributed by him to the greater importunity of the vicious, which generally prevails over the retiring bashfulness of the virtuous indigent. There was one circumstance about the charity of his Lordship, which was still more impressed upon his mind: all those upon whom it was bestowed, inevitably found that there was a curse upon it, for they

were all either led to the scaffold, or sunk to the lowest and the
most abject misery. At Brussels and other towns through which
they passed, Aubrey was surprized at the apparent eagerness
with which his companion sought for the centres of all fashionable vice; there he entered into all the spirit of the faro table:[12] he
betted, and always gambled with success, except where the
known sharper was his antagonist, and then he lost even more
than he gained; but it was always with the same unchanging
face, with which he generally watched the society around: it was
not, however, so when he encountered the rash youthful novice,
or the luckless father of a numerous family; then his very wish
seemed fortune's law—this apparent abstractedness of mind
was laid aside, and his eyes sparkled with more fire than that
of the cat whilst dallying with the half-dead mouse. In every
town, he left the formerly affluent youth, torn from the circle he
adorned, cursing, in the solitude of a dungeon, the fate that had
drawn him within the reach of this fiend: whilst many a father
sat frantic, amidst the speaking looks of mute hungry children,
without a single farthing of his late immense wealth, wherewith
to buy even sufficient to satisfy their present craving. Yet he took
no money from the gambling table; but immediately lost, to the
ruiner of many, the last gilder[13] he had just snatched from the
convulsive grasp of the innocent: this might but be the result of
a certain degree of knowledge, which was not, however, capable
of combating the cunning of the more experienced. Aubrey
often wished to represent this to his friend, and beg him to re-
sign that charity and pleasure which proved the ruin of all, and
did not tend to his own profit;—but he delayed it—for each day
he hoped his friend would give him some opportunity of speaking frankly and openly to him; however, this never occurred.
Lord Ruthven in his carriage,[14] and amidst the various wild and
rich scenes of nature, was always the same: his eye spoke less

than his lip; and though Aubrey was near the object of his curiosity, he obtained no greater gratification from it than the constant excitement of vainly wishing to break that mystery, which to his exalted imagination began to assume the appearance of something supernatural.

They soon arrived at Rome, and Aubrey for a time lost sight of his companion; he left him in daily attendance upon the morning circle of an Italian countess, whilst he went in search of the memorials of another almost deserted city. Whilst he was thus engaged, letters arrived from England, which he opened with eager impatience; the first was from his sister, breathing nothing but affection; the others were from his guardians, the latter astonished him; if it had before entered into his imagination that there was an evil power resident in his companion, these seemed to give him almost sufficient reason for the belief. His guardians insisted upon his immediately leaving his friend, and urged, that his character was dreadfully vicious, for that the possession of irresistible powers of seduction, rendered his licentious habits more dangerous to society. It had been discovered, that his contempt for the adultress had not originated in hatred of her character; but that he had required, to enhance his gratification, that his victim, the partner of his guilt, should be hurled from the pinnacle of unsullied virtue, down to the lowest abyss of infamy and degradation: in fine, that all those females whom he had sought, apparently on account of their virtue, had, since his departure, thrown even the mask aside, and had not scrupled to expose the whole deformity of their vices to the public gaze.

Aubrey determined upon leaving one, whose character had not yet shown a single bright point on which to rest the eye. He resolved to invent some plausible pretext for abandoning him altogether, purposing, in the mean while, to watch him more closely, and to let no slight circumstances pass by unnoticed. He entered into the same circle, and soon perceived, that his Lordship was endeavouring to work upon the inexperience of the daughter of the lady whose house he chiefly frequented. In Italy, it is seldom that an unmarried female is met with in society; he was therefore obliged to carry on his plans in secret; but Aubrey's eye followed him in all his windings, and soon discovered that an assignation had been appointed, which would most likely end in the ruin of an innocent, though thoughtless girl. Losing no time, he entered the apartment of Lord Ruthven, and abruptly asked him his intentions with respect to the lady, informing him at the same time that he was aware of his being about to meet her that very night. Lord Ruthven answered, that his intentions were such as he supposed all would have upon such an occasion; and upon being pressed whether he intended to marry her, merely laughed. Aubrey retired; and, immediately writing a note, to say, that from that moment he must decline accompanying his Lordship in the remainder of their proposed tour, he ordered his servant to seek other apartments, and calling upon the mother of the lady, informed her of all he knew, not only with regard to her daughter, but also concerning the character of his Lordship. The assignation was prevented. Lord Ruthven next day merely sent his servant to notify his complete assent to a separation; but did not hint any suspicion of his plans having been foiled by Aubrey's interposition.

Having left Rome, Aubrey directed his steps towards Greece, and crossing the Peninsula, soon found himself at Athens. He then fixed his residence in the house of a Greek; and soon occupied himself in tracing the faded records of ancient glory upon monuments that apparently, ashamed of chronicling the deeds of freemen only before slaves, had hidden themselves beneath the sheltering soil or many coloured lichen. Under the same roof as himself, existed a being, so beautiful and delicate, that she might have formed the model for a painter wishing to pourtray on canvass the promised hope of the faithful in Mahomet's paradise, save that her eyes spoke too much mind for any one to think she could belong to those who had no souls. As she danced upon the plain, or tripped along the mountain's side, one would have thought the gazelle[15] a poor type of her beauties; for who would have exchanged her eye, apparently the eye of animated nature, for that sleepy luxurious look of the animal suited but to the taste of an epicure. The light step of Ianthe[16] often accompanied Aubrey in his search after antiquities, and often would the unconscious girl, engaged in the pursuit of a Kashmere butterfly,[17] show the whole beauty of her form, floating as it were upon the wind, to the eager gaze of him, who forgot the letters he had just decyphered upon an almost effaced tablet, in the contemplation of her sylph-like figure. Often would her tresses falling, as she flitted around, exhibit in the sun's ray such delicately brilliant and swiftly fading hues, as might well excuse the forgetfulness of the antiquary, who let escape from his mind the very object he had before thought of vital importance to the proper interpretation of a passage in Pausanias.[18] But why attempt to describe charms which all feel, but none can appreciate?—It was innocence, youth, and beauty, unaffected by crowded drawing-rooms and stifling balls. Whilst he drew those remains of which he wished to preserve a memorial for his future hours, she would stand by, and watch the magic effects of his pencil, in tracing the scenes of her native place; she would then describe to him the circling dance upon the open plain, would paint to him in all the glowing colours of youthful memory, the marriage pomp she remembered viewing in her infancy; and then, turning to subjects that had evidently made a greater impression upon her mind, would tell him all the supernatural tales of her nurse. Her

earnestness and apparent belief of what she narrated, excited
the interest even of Aubrey; and often as she told him the tale of
the living vampyre, who had passed years amidst his friends,
and dearest ties, forced every year, by feeding upon the life of a
lovely female to prolong his existence for the ensuing months,
his blood would run cold, whilst he attempted to laugh her out
of such idle and horrible fantasies; but Ianthe cited to him the
names of old men, who had at last detected one living among
themselves, after several of their near relatives and children had
been found marked with the stamp of the fiend's appetite; and
when she found him so incredulous, she begged of him to believe her, for it had been remarked, that those who had dared to
question their existence, always had some proof given, which
obliged them, with grief and heartbreaking, to confess it was
true. She detailed to him the traditional appearance of these
monsters, and his horror was increased, by hearing a pretty ac-
curate description of Lord Ruthven; he, however, still persisted
in persuading her, that there could be no truth in her fears,
though at the same time he wondered at the many coincidences
which had all tended to excite a belief in the supernatural power
of Lord Ruthven.

Aubrey began to attach himself more and more to Ianthe; her
innocence, so contrasted with all the affected virtues of the
women among whom he had sought for his vision of romance,
won his heart; and while he ridiculed the idea of a young man
of English habits, marrying an uneducated Greek girl, still he
found himself more and more attached to the almost fairy form
before him. He would tear himself at times from her, and, forming a plan for some antiquarian research, he would depart, determined not to return until his object was attained; but he
always found it impossible to fix his attention upon the ruins
around him, whilst in his mind he retained an image that seemed

alone the rightful possessor of his thoughts. Ianthe was unconscious of his love, and was ever the same frank infantile being he had first known. She always seemed to part from him with reluctance; but it was because she had no longer any one with whom she could visit her favourite haunts, whilst her guardian was occupied in sketching or uncovering some fragment which had yet escaped the destructive hand of time. She had appealed to her parents on the subject of Vampyres, and they both, with several present, affirmed their existence, pale with horror at the very name. Soon after, Aubrey determined to proceed upon one of his excursions, which was to detain him for a few hours; when they heard the name of the place, they all at once begged of him not to return at night, as he must necessarily pass through a wood, where no Greek would ever remain, after the day had closed, upon any consideration. They described it as the resort of the vampyres in their nocturnal orgies,[19] and denounced the most heavy evils as impending upon him who dared to cross their path. Aubrey made light of their representations, and tried to laugh them out of the idea; but when he saw them shudder at his daring thus to mock a superior, infernal power, the very name of which apparently made their blood freeze, he was silent.

Next morning Aubrey set off upon his excursion unattended; he was surprised to observe the melancholy face of his host, and was concerned to find that his words, mocking the belief of those horrible fiends, had inspired them with such terror. When he was about to depart, Ianthe came to the side of his horse, and earnestly begged of him to return, ere night allowed the power of these beings to be put in action;—he promised. He was, however, so occupied in his research, that he did not perceive that day-light would soon end, and that in the horizon there was one of those specks which, in the warmer climates, so rapidly gather into a tremendous mass, and pour all their rage upon the devoted country.—He at last, however, mounted his horse, determined to make up by speed for his delay: but it was too late. Twilight, in these southern climates, is almost unknown; immediately the sun sets, night begins: and ere he had advanced far, the power of the storm was above—its echoing thunders had scarcely an interval of rest—its thick heavy rain forced its way through the canopying foliage, whilst the blue forked lightning seemed to fall and radiate at his very feet. Suddenly his horse took fright, and he was carried with dreadful rapidity through the entangled forest. The animal at last, through fatigue, stopped, and he found, by the glare of lightning, that he was in the neighbourhood of a hovel that hardly lifted itself up from the masses of dead leaves and brushwood which surrounded it. Dismounting, he approached, hoping to find some one to guide him to the town, or at least trusting to obtain shelter from the pelting of the storm. As he approached, the thunders, for a moment silent, allowed him to hear the dreadful shrieks of a woman mingling with the stifled, exultant mockery of a laugh, continued in one almost unbroken sound;—he was startled: but, roused by the thunder which again rolled over his head, he, with a sudden effort, forced open the door of the hut. He found himself in utter darkness: the sound, however, guided him. He was apparently unperceived; for, though he called, still the sounds continued, and no notice was taken of him. He found himself in contact with some one, whom he immediately seized; when a voice cried, 'Again baffled!' to which a loud laugh succeeded; and he felt himself grappled by one whose strength seemed superhuman: determined to sell his life as dearly as he could, he struggled; but it was in vain: he was lifted from his feet and hurled with enormous force against the ground:—his enemy threw himself upon him, and kneeling upon his breast, had placed his

hands upon his throat—when the glare of many torches penetrating through the hole that gave light in the day, disturbed
him;—he instantly rose, and, leaving his prey, rushed through
the door, and in a moment the crashing of the branches, as he
broke through the wood, was no longer heard. The storm was
now still; and Aubrey, incapable of moving, was soon heard by
those without. They entered; the light of their torches fell upon
the mud walls, and the thatch loaded on every individual straw
with heavy flakes of soot. At the desire of Aubrey they searched
for her who had attracted him by her cries; he was again left in
darkness; but what was his horror, when the light of the torches
once more burst upon him, to perceive the airy form of his fair
conductress brought in a lifeless corse. He shut his eyes, hoping
that it was but a vision arising from his disturbed imagination;
but he again saw the same form, when he unclosed them,
stretched by his side. There was no colour upon her cheek, not
even upon her lip; yet there was a stillness about her face that
seemed almost as attaching as the life that once dwelt there:—
upon her neck and breast was blood, and upon her throat were
the marks of teeth having opened the vein:—to this the men
pointed, crying, simultaneously struck with horror, 'A Vampyre!
a Vampyre!' A litter was quickly formed, and Aubrey was laid
by the side of her who had lately been to him the object of so
many bright and fairy visions, now fallen with the flower of life
that had died within her. He knew not what his thoughts were—
his mind was benumbed and seemed to shun reflection, and take
refuge in vacancy—he held almost unconsciously in his hand a
naked dagger of a particular construction, which had been
found in the hut. They were soon met by different parties who
had been engaged in the search of her whom a mother had
missed. Their lamentable cries, as they approached the city,
forewarned the parents of some dreadful catastrophe.—To de-

scribe their grief would be impossible; but when they ascertained the cause of their child's death, they looked at Aubrey and pointed to the corse. They were inconsolable; both died broken-hearted.

Aubrey being put to bed was seized with a most violent fever, and was often delirious; in these intervals he would call upon Lord Ruthven and upon Ianthe—by some unaccountable combination he seemed to beg of his former companion to spare the being he loved. At other times he would imprecate maledictions upon his head, and curse him as her destroyer. Lord Ruthven chanced at this time to arrive at Athens, and, from whatever motive, upon hearing of the state of Aubrey, immediately placed himself in the same house, and became his constant attendant. When the latter recovered from his delirium, he was horrified and startled at the sight of him whose image he had now combined with that of a Vampyre; but Lord Ruthven, by his kind words, implying almost repentance for the fault that had caused their separation, and still more by the attention, anxiety, and care which he showed, soon reconciled him to his presence. His lordship seemed quite changed; he no longer appeared that apathetic being who had so astonished Aubrey; but as soon as his convalescence began to be rapid, he again gradually retired into the same state of mind, and Aubrey perceived no difference from the former man, except that at times he was surprised to meet his gaze fixed intently upon him, with a smile of malicious exultation playing upon his lips: he knew not why, but this smile haunted him. During the last stage of the invalid's recovery, Lord Ruthven was apparently engaged in watching the tideless waves[20] raised by the cooling breeze, or in marking the progress of those orbs, circling, like our world, the moveless sun;— indeed, he appeared to wish to avoid the eyes of all.

Aubrey's mind, by this shock, was much weakened, and that

elasticity of spirit which had once so distinguished him now seemed to have fled for ever. He was now as much a lover of solitude and silence as Lord Ruthven; but much as he wished for solitude, his mind could not find it in the neighbourhood of Athens; if he sought it amidst the ruins he had formerly frequented, Ianthe's form stood by his side—if he sought it in the woods, her light step would appear wandering amidst the underwood, in quest of the modest violet; then suddenly turning round, would show, to his wild imagination, her pale face and wounded throat, with a meek smile upon her lips. He determined to fly scenes, every feature of which created such bitter associations in his mind. He proposed to Lord Ruthven, to whom he held himself bound by the tender care he had taken of him during his illness, that they should visit those parts of Greece neither had yet seen. They travelled in every direction, and sought every spot to which a recollection could be attached: but though they thus hastened from place to place, yet they seemed not to heed what they gazed upon. They heard much of robbers, but they gradually began to slight these reports, which they imagined were only the invention of individuals, whose interest it was to excite the generosity of those whom they defended from pretended dangers. In consequence of thus neglecting the advice of the inhabitants, on one occasion they travelled with only a few guards, more to serve as guides than as a defence. Upon entering, however, a narrow defile,[21] at the bottom of which was the bed of a torrent, with large masses of rock brought down from the neighbouring precipices, they had reason to repent their negligence; for scarcely were the whole of the party engaged in the narrow pass, when they were startled by the whistling of bullets close to their heads, and by the echoed report of several guns. In an instant their guards had left them, and, placing themselves behind rocks, had begun to fire in the direction whence the report came.

Lord Ruthven and Aubrey, imitating their example, retired for a
moment behind the sheltering turn of the defile: but ashamed of
being thus detained by a foe, who with insulting shouts bade
them advance, and being exposed to unresisting slaughter, if
any of the robbers should climb above and take them in the rear,
they determined at once to rush forward in search of the enemy.
Hardly had they lost the shelter of the rock, when Lord Ruthven
received a shot in the shoulder, which brought him to the
ground. Aubrey hastened to his assistance; and, no longer heed-
ing the contest or his own peril, was soon surprised by seeing
the robbers' faces around him—his guards having, upon Lord
Ruthven's being wounded, immediately thrown up their arms
and surrendered.

By promises of great reward, Aubrey soon induced them to
convey his wounded friend to a neighbouring cabin; and having
agreed upon a ransom, he was no more disturbed by their
presence—they being content merely to guard the entrance till
their comrade should return with the promised sum, for which
he had an order.[22] Lord Ruthven's strength rapidly decreased; in
two days mortification ensued, and death seemed advancing
with hasty steps. His conduct and appearance had not changed;
he seemed as unconscious of pain as he had been of the objects
about him: but towards the close of the last evening, his mind
became apparently uneasy, and his eye often fixed upon Aubrey,
who was induced to offer his assistance with more than usual
earnestness——'Assist me! you may save me—you may do more
than that—I mean not my life, I heed the death of my existence
as little as that of the passing day; but you may save my honour,
your friend's honour.'—'How? tell me how? I would do any
thing,' replied Aubrey.—'I need but little—my life ebbs apace—
I cannot explain the whole—but if you would conceal all you
know of me, my honour were free from stain in the world's

mouth—and if my death were unknown for some time in England—I—I—but life.'—'It shall not be known.'—'Swear!' cried the dying man, raising himself with exultant violence, 'Swear by all your soul reveres, by all your nature fears, swear that for a year and a day you will not impart your knowledge of my crimes or death to any living being in any way, whatever may happen, or whatever you may see.'—His eyes seemed bursting from their sockets: 'I swear!' said Aubrey; he sunk laughing upon his pillow, and breathed no more.

Aubrey retired to rest, but did not sleep; the many circumstances attending his acquaintance with this man rose upon his mind, and he knew not why; when he remembered his oath a cold shivering came over him, as if from the presentiment of something horrible awaiting him. Rising early in the morning, he was about to enter the hovel in which he had left the corpse, when a robber met him, and informed him that it was no longer there, having been conveyed by himself and comrades, upon his retiring, to the pinnacle of a neighbouring mount, according to a promise they had given his lordship, that it should be exposed to the first cold ray of the moon that rose after his death. Aubrey astonished,[23] and taking several of the men, determined to go and bury it upon the spot where it lay. But, when he had mounted to the summit he found no trace of either the corpse or the clothes, though the robbers swore they pointed out the identical rock on which they had laid the body. For a time his mind was bewildered in conjectures, but he at last returned, convinced that they had buried the corpse for the sake of the clothes.

Weary of a country in which he had met with such terrible misfortunes, and in which all apparently conspired to heighten that superstitious melancholy that had seized upon his mind, he resolved to leave it, and soon arrived at Smyrna.[24] While waiting for a vessel to convey him to Otranto,[25] or to Naples, he occu-

pied himself in arranging those effects he had with him belong-
ing to Lord Ruthven. Amongst other things there was a case
containing several weapons of offence, more or less adapted to
ensure the death of the victim. There were several daggers and
ataghans.[26] Whilst turning them over, and examining their curious forms, what was his surprise at finding a sheath apparently
ornamented in the same style as the dagger discovered in the
fatal hut—he shuddered—hastening to gain further proof, he
found the weapon, and his horror may be imagined when he discovered that it fitted, though peculiarly shaped, the sheath he
held in his hand. His eyes seemed to need no further certainty—
they seemed gazing to be bound to the dagger; yet still he wished
to disbelieve; but the particular form, the same varying tints
upon the haft and sheath were alike in splendour on both, and
left no room for doubt; there were also drops of blood on each.

He left Smyrna, and on his way home, at Rome, his first inquiries were concerning the lady he had attempted to snatch
from Lord Ruthven's seductive arts. Her parents were in distress, their fortune ruined, and she had not been heard of since
the departure of his lordship. Aubrey's mind became almost
broken under so many repeated horrors; he was afraid that this
lady had fallen a victim to the destroyer of Ianthe. He became
morose and silent; and his only occupation consisted in urging
the speed of the postilions, as if he were going to save the life of
some one he held dear. He arrived at Calais; a breeze, which
seemed obedient to his will, soon wafted him to the English
shores; and he hastened to the mansion of his fathers, and there,
for a moment, appeared to lose, in the embraces and caresses of
his sister, all memory of the past. If she before, by her infantine[27]
caresses, had gained his affection, now that the woman began to
appear, she was still more attaching as a companion.

Miss Aubrey had not that winning grace which gains the gaze

and applause of the drawing-room assemblies. There was none
of that light brilliancy which only exists in the heated atmosphere of a crowded apartment. Her blue eye was never lit up by
the levity of the mind beneath. There was a melancholy charm
about it which did not seem to arise from misfortune, but from
some feeling within, that appeared to indicate a soul conscious
of a brighter realm. Her step was not that light footing, which
strays where'er a butterfly or a colour may attract—it was sedate
and pensive. When alone, her face was never brightened by the
smile of joy; but when her brother breathed to her his affection,
and would in her presence forget those griefs she knew destroyed his rest, who would have exchanged her smile for that of
the voluptuary?[28] It seemed as if those eyes,—that face were
then playing in the light of their own native sphere. She was yet
only eighteen, and had not been presented to the world, it having been thought by her guardians more fit that her presentation
should be delayed until her brother's return from the continent,
when he might be her protector. It was now, therefore, resolved
that the next drawing-room,[29] which was fast approaching,
should be the epoch of her entry into the 'busy scene.'[30] Aubrey
would rather have remained in the mansion of his fathers, and
fed upon the melancholy which overpowered him. He could not
feel interest about the frivolities of fashionable strangers, when
his mind had been so torn by the events he had witnessed; but
he determined to sacrifice his own comfort to the protection of
his sister. They soon arrived in town, and prepared for the next
day, which had been announced as a drawing-room.

The crowd was excessive—a drawing-room had not been
held for a long time, and all who were anxious to bask in the
smile of royalty, hastened thither. Aubrey was there with his sister. While he was standing in a corner by himself, heedless of all
around him, engaged in the remembrance that the first time he

had seen Lord Ruthven was in that very place—he felt himself suddenly seized by the arm, and a voice he recognized too well, sounded in his ear—'Remember your oath.' He had hardly courage to turn, fearful of seeing a spectre that would blast him, when he perceived, at a little distance, the same figure which had attracted his notice on this spot upon his first entry into society. He gazed till his limbs almost refusing to bear their weight, he was obliged to take the arm of a friend, and forcing a passage through the crowd, he threw himself into his carriage, and was driven home. He paced the room with hurried steps, and fixed his hands upon his head, as if he were afraid his thoughts were bursting from his brain. Lord Ruthven again before him—circumstances started up in dreadful array—the dagger—his oath.—He roused himself, he could not believe it possible—the dead rise again!—He thought his imagination had conjured up the image his mind was resting upon. It was impossible that it could be real—he determined, therefore, to go again into society; for though he attempted to ask concerning Lord Ruthven, the name hung upon his lips, and he could not succeed in gaining information. He went a few nights after with his sister to the assembly of a near relation. Leaving her under the protection of a matron, he retired into a recess, and there gave himself up to his own devouring thoughts. Perceiving, at last, that many were leaving, he roused himself, and entering another room, found his sister surrounded by several, apparently in earnest conversation; he attempted to pass and get near her, when one, whom he requested to move, turned round, and revealed to him those features he most abhorred. He sprang forward, seized his sister's arm, and, with hurried step, forced her towards the street: at the door he found himself impeded by the crowd of servants who were waiting for their lords; and while he was engaged in passing them, he again heard that voice whisper

close to him—'Remember your oath!'—He did not dare to turn,
but, hurrying his sister, soon reached home.

Aubrey became almost distracted. If before his mind had been
absorbed by one subject, how much more completely was it en-
grossed, now that the certainty of the monster's living again
pressed upon his thoughts. His sister's attentions were now un-
heeded, and it was in vain that she intreated him to explain to
her what had caused his abrupt conduct. He only uttered a few
words, and those terrified her. The more he thought, the more he
was bewildered. His oath startled him;—was he then to allow
this monster to roam, bearing ruin upon his breath, amidst all he
held dear, and not avert its progress? His very sister might have
been touched by him. But even if he were to break his oath, and
disclose his suspicions, who would believe him? He thought of
employing his own hand to free the world from such a wretch;
but death, he remembered, had been already mocked. For days
he remained in this state; shut up in his room, he saw no one, and
eat only when his sister came, who, with eyes streaming with
tears, besought him, for her sake, to support nature.[31] At last, no
longer capable of bearing stillness and solitude, he left his house,
roamed from street to street, anxious to fly that image which
haunted him. His dress became neglected, and he wandered, as
often exposed to the noon-day sun as to the midnight damps. He
was no longer to be recognized; at first he returned with the evening to the house; but at last he laid him down to rest wherever
fatigue overtook him. His sister, anxious for his safety, employed
people to follow him; but they were soon distanced by him who
fled from a pursuer swifter than any—from thought. His conduct, however, suddenly changed. Struck with the idea that he
left by his absence the whole of his friends, with a fiend amongst
them, of whose presence they were unconscious, he determined
to enter again into society, and watch him closely, anxious to

forewarn, in spite of his oath, all whom Lord Ruthven approached with intimacy. But when he entered into a room, his haggard and suspicious looks were so striking, his inward shudderings so visible, that his sister was at last obliged to beg of him to abstain from seeking, for her sake, a society which affected him so strongly. When, however, remonstrance proved unavailing, the guardians thought proper to interpose, and, fearing that his mind was becoming alienated, they thought it high time to resume again that trust which had been before imposed upon them by Aubrey's parents.

Desirous of saving him from the injuries and sufferings he had daily encountered in his wanderings, and of preventing him from exposing to the general eye those marks of what they considered folly, they engaged a physician to reside in the house, and take constant care of him. He hardly appeared to notice it, so completely was his mind absorbed by one terrible subject. His incoherence became at last so great, that he was confined to his chamber. There he would often lie for days, incapable of being roused. He had become emaciated, his eyes had attained a glassy lustre;—the only sign of affection and recollection remaining displayed itself upon the entry of his sister; then he would sometimes start, and, seizing her hands, with looks that severely afflicted her, he would desire her not to touch him. 'Oh, do not touch him—if your love for me is aught, do not go near him!' When, however, she inquired to whom he referred, his only answer was, 'True! true!' and again he sank into a state, whence not even she could rouse him. This lasted many months: gradually, however, as the year was passing, his incoherences became less frequent, and his mind threw off a portion of its gloom, whilst his guardians observed, that several times in the day he would count upon his fingers a definite number, and then smile.

The time had nearly elapsed, when, upon the last day of the

year, one of his guardians entering his room, began to converse
with his physician upon the melancholy circumstance of Aubrey's being in so awful a situation, when his sister was going
next day to be married. Instantly Aubrey's attention was attracted; he asked anxiously to whom. Glad of this mark of re-
turning intellect, of which they feared he had been deprived,
they mentioned the name of the Earl of Marsden. Thinking this
was a young Earl whom he had met with in society, Aubrey
seemed pleased, and astonished them still more by his expressing his intention to be present at the nuptials, and desiring to see
his sister. They answered not, but in a few minutes his sister was
with him. He was apparently again capable of being affected by
the influence of her lovely smile; for he pressed her to his breast,
and kissed her cheek, wet with tears, flowing at the thought of
her brother's being once more alive to the feelings of affection.
He began to speak with all his wonted warmth, and to congratulate her upon her marriage with a person so distinguished for
rank and every accomplishment; when he suddenly perceived a
locket upon her breast; opening it, what was his surprise at be-
holding the features of the monster who had so long influenced
his life. He seized the portrait in a paroxysm of rage, and tram-
pled it under foot. Upon her asking him why he thus destroyed
the resemblance of her future husband, he looked as if he did
not understand her—then seizing her hands, and gazing on her
with a frantic expression of countenance, he bade her swear that
she would never wed this monster, for he——But he could not
advance—it seemed as if that voice again bade him remember
his oath—he turned suddenly round, thinking Lord Ruthven
was near him but saw no one. In the meantime the guardians
and physician, who had heard the whole, and thought this was
but a return of his disorder, entered, and forcing him from Miss
Aubrey, desired her to leave him. He fell upon his knees to them,

he implored, he begged of them to delay but for one day. They, attributing this to the insanity they imagined had taken possession of his mind, endeavoured to pacify him, and retired.

Lord Ruthven had called the morning after the drawing-room, and had been refused with every one else. When he heard of Aubrey's ill health, he readily understood himself to be the cause of it; but when he learned that he was deemed insane, his exultation and pleasure could hardly be concealed from those among whom he had gained this information. He hastened to the house of his former companion, and, by constant attendance, and the pretence of great affection for the brother and interest in his fate, he gradually won the ear of Miss Aubrey. Who could resist his power? His tongue had dangers and toils to recount—could speak of himself as of an individual having no sympathy with any being on the crowded earth, save with her to whom he addressed himself;—could tell how, since he knew her, his existence had begun to seem worthy of preservation, if it were merely that he might listen to her soothing accents;—in fine, he knew so well how to use the serpent's art,[32] or such was the will of fate, that he gained her affections. The title of the elder branch falling at length to him, he obtained an important embassy, which served as an excuse for hastening the marriage, (in spite of her brother's deranged state,) which was to take place the very day before his departure for the continent.

Aubrey, when he was left by the physician and his guardians, attempted to bribe the servants, but in vain. He asked for pen and paper; it was given him; he wrote a letter to his sister, conjuring[33] her, as she valued her own happiness, her own honour, and the honour of those now in the grave, who once held her in their arms as their hope and the hope of their house, to delay but for a few hours that marriage, on which he denounced the most heavy curses. The servants promised they would deliver it; but giving it to the physician, he thought it better not to harass any more the mind of Miss Aubrey by, what he considered, the ravings of a maniac. Night passed on without rest to the busy inmates of the house; and Aubrey heard, with a horror that may more easily be conceived than described, the notes of busy preparation. Morning came, and the sound of carriages broke upon his ear. Aubrey grew almost frantic. The curiosity of the servants at last overcame their vigilance, they gradually stole away, leaving him in the custody of an helpless old woman. He seized the opportunity, with one bound was out of the room, and in a moment found himself in the apartment where all were nearly assembled. Lord Ruthven was the first to perceive him: he immediately approached, and, taking his arm by force, hurried him from the room, speechless with rage. When on the staircase, Lord Ruthven whispered in his ear—'Remember your oath, and know, if not my bride to day, your sister is dishonoured. Women are frail!' So saying, he pushed him towards his attendants, who, roused by the old woman, had come in search of him. Aubrey could no longer support himself; his rage not finding vent, had broken a blood-vessel, and he was conveyed to bed. This was not mentioned to his sister, who was not present when he entered, as the physician was afraid of agitating her. The marriage was solemnized, and the bride and bridegroom left London.

Aubrey's weakness increased; the effusion of blood produced symptoms of the near approach of death. He desired his sister's guardians might be called, and when the midnight hour had struck, he related composedly what the reader has perused—he died immediately after.

The guardians hastened to protect Miss Aubrey; but when they arrived, it was too late. Lord Ruthven had disappeared, and Aubrey's sister had glutted the thirst of a VAMPYRE!

Carmilla

SHERIDAN Le FANU

Prologue

Upon a paper attached to the Narrative which follows, Doctor Hesselius has written a rather elaborate note, which he accompanies with a reference to his Essay on the strange subject which the MS. illuminates.

This mysterious subject, he treats, in that Essay, with his usual learning and acumen, and with remarkable directness and condensation. It will form but one volume of the series of that extraordinary man's collected papers.

As I publish the case, in this volume, simply to interest the 'laity,' I shall forestall the intelligent lady, who relates it, in nothing; and after due consideration, I have determined, therefore, to abstain from presenting any *précis* of the learned Doctor's reasoning, or extract from his statement on a subject which he describes as 'involving, not improbably, some of the profoundest arcana of our dual existence, and its intermediates'.[1]

I was anxious, on discovering this paper, to re-open the correspondence commenced by Doctor Hesselius, so many years before, with a person so clever and careful as his informant seems to have been. Much to my regret, however, I found that she had died in the interval.

She, probably, could have added little to the Narrative which she communicates in the following pages, with, so far as I can pronounce, such conscientious particularity.

CHAPTER I.

An Early Fright.

In Styria,[1] we, though by no means magnificent people, inhabit a castle, or schloss. A small income, in that part of the world, goes a great way. Eight or nine hundred a year does wonders. Scantily enough ours would have answered among wealthy people at home. My father is English, and I bear an English name, although I never saw England. But here, in this lonely and primitive place, where everything is so marvellously cheap, I really don't see how ever so much more money would at all materially add to our comforts, or even luxuries.

My father was in the Austrian service,[2] and retired upon a pension and his patrimony, and purchased this feudal residence, and the small estate on which it stands, a bargain.

Nothing can be more picturesque or solitary. It stands on a slight eminence in a forest. The road, very old and narrow, passes in front of its drawbridge, never raised in my time, and its moat, stocked with perch, and sailed over by many swans, and floating on its surface white fleets of water-lilies.

Over all this the schloss shows its many-windowed front; its towers, and its Gothic chapel.

The forest opens in an irregular and very picturesque glade before its gate, and at the right a steep Gothic bridge carries the road over a stream that winds in deep shadow through the wood.

I have said that this is a very lonely place. Judge whether I say truth. Looking from the hall door towards the road, the forest in which our castle stands extends fifteen miles to the right, and twelve to the left. The nearest inhabited village is about seven of your English miles to the left. The nearest inhabited schloss of any historic associations, is that of old General Spielsdorf, nearly twenty miles away to the right.

I have said 'the nearest *inhabited* village,' because there is, only three miles westward, that is to say in the direction of General Spielsdorf's schloss, a ruined village, with its quaint little church, now roofless, in the aisle of which are the mouldering tombs of the proud family of Karnstein, now extinct, who once owned the equally desolate château which, in the thick of the forest, overlooks the silent ruins of the town.

Respecting the cause of the desertion of this striking and melancholy spot, there is a legend which I shall relate to you another time.

I must tell you now, how very small is the party who constitute the inhabitants of our castle. I don't include servants, or those dependents who occupy rooms in the buildings attached to the schloss. Listen, and wonder! My father, who is the kindest man on earth, but growing old; and I, at the date of my story, only nineteen. Eight years have passed since then. I and my father constituted the family at the schloss. My mother, a Styrian lady, died in my infancy, but I had a good-natured governess, who had been with me from, I might almost say, my infancy. I could not remember the time when her fat, benignant face was not a familiar picture in my memory. This was Madame Perrodon, a native of Berne,[3] whose care and good nature in part supplied to me the loss of my mother, whom I do not even remember, so early I lost her. She made a third at our little dinner party. There was a fourth, Mademoiselle De Lafontaine, a lady such as you term, I believe, a 'finishing governess.' She spoke French and German, Madame Perrodon French and broken English, to which my father and I added English, which, partly to prevent its becoming a lost language among us, and partly from patriotic motives, we spoke every day. The consequence was a Babel,[4] at which strangers used to laugh, and which I shall make no attempt to reproduce in this narrative. And there were two or three young lady friends besides, pretty nearly of my own age, who were occasional visitors, for longer or shorter terms; and these visits I sometimes returned.

These were our regular social resources; but of course there were chance visits from 'neighbours' of only five or six leagues distance. My life was, notwithstanding, rather a solitary one, I can assure you.

My gouvernantes[5] had just so much control over me as you might conjecture such sage persons would have in the case of a rather spoiled girl, whose only parent allowed her pretty nearly her own way in everything.

The first occurrence in my existence, which produced a terrible impression upon my mind, which, in fact, never has been effaced, was one of the very earliest incidents of my life which I can recollect. Some people will think it so trifling that it should not be recorded here. You will see, however, by-and-bye, why I mention it. The nursery, as it was called, though I had it all to myself, was a large room in the upper story of the castle, with a steep oak roof. I can't have been more than six years old, when one night I awoke, and looking round the room from my bed, failed to see the nursery-maid. Neither was my nurse there; and I thought myself alone. I was not frightened, for I was one of those happy children who are studiously kept in ignorance of ghost stories, of

fairy tales, and of all such lore as makes us cover up our heads
when the door creeks suddenly, or the flicker of an expiring candle makes the shadow of a bed-post dance upon the wall, nearer
to our faces. I was vexed and insulted at finding myself, as I conceived, neglected, and I began to whimper, preparatory to a
hearty bout of roaring; when to my surprise, I saw a solemn, but
very pretty face looking at me from the side of the bed. It was that
of a young lady who was kneeling, with her hands under the cov-
erlet. I looked at her with a kind of pleased wonder, and ceased
whimpering. She caressed me with her hands, and lay down
beside me on the bed, and drew me towards her, smiling; I felt
immediately delightfully soothed, and fell asleep again. I was
wakened by a sensation as if two needles ran into my breast very
deep at the same moment, and I cried loudly. The lady started
back, with her eyes fixed on me, and then slipped down upon the
floor, and, as I thought, hid herself under the bed.

I was now for the first time frightened, and I yelled with all
my might and main. Nurse, nursery-maid, housekeeper, all
came running in, and hearing my story, they made light of it,
soothing me all they could meanwhile. But, child as I was, I
could perceive that their faces were pale with an unwonted look
of anxiety, and I saw them look under the bed, and about the
room, and peep under tables and pluck open cupboards; and the
housekeeper whispered to the nurse: 'Lay your hand along that
hollow in the bed; someone *did* lie there, so sure as you did not;
the place is still warm.'

I remember the nursery-maid petting me, and all three examining my chest, where I told them I felt the puncture, and pro-
nouncing that there was no sign visible that any such thing had
happened to me.

The housekeeper and the two other servants who were in
charge of the nursery, remained sitting up all night; and from

that time a servant always sat up in the nursery until I was about fourteen.

I was very nervous for a long time after this. A doctor was called in, he was pallid and elderly. How well I remember his long saturnine face, slightly pitted with small-pox, and his chestnut wig. For a good while, every second day, he came and gave me medicine, which of course I hated.

The morning after I saw this apparition I was in a state of terror, and could not bear to be left alone, daylight though it was, for a moment.

I remember my father coming up and standing at the bedside, and talking cheerfully, and asking the nurse a number of questions, and laughing very heartily at one of the answers; and patting me on the shoulder, and kissing me, and telling me not to be frightened, that it was nothing but a dream and could not hurt me.

But I was not comforted, for I knew the visit of the strange woman was *not* a dream; and I was *awfully* frightened.

I was a little consoled by the nursery-maid's assuring me that it was she who had come and looked at me, and lain down beside me in the bed, and that I must have been half-dreaming not to have known her face. But this, though supported by the nurse, did not quite satisfy me.

I remember, in the course of that day, a venerable old man, in a black cassock, coming into the room with the nurse and housekeeper, and talking a little to them, and very kindly to me; his face was very sweet and gentle, and he told me they were going to pray, and joined my hands together, and desired me to say, softly, while they were praying, 'Lord hear all good prayers for us, for Jesus' sake.' I think these were the very words, for I often repeated them to myself, and my nurse used for years to make me say them in my prayers.

I remember so well the thoughtful sweet face of that white-haired old man, in his black cassock, as he stood in that rude, lofty, brown room, with the clumsy furniture of a fashion three hundred years old, about him, and the scanty light entering its shadowy atmosphere through the small lattice. He kneeled, and the three women with him, and he prayed aloud with an earnest quavering voice for, what appeared to me, a long time. I forget all my life preceding that event, and for some time after it is all obscure also, but the scenes I have just described stand out vivid as the isolated pictures of the phantasmagoria[6] surrounded by darkness.

CHAPTER II

A Guest.

I am now going to tell you something so strange that it will require all your faith in my veracity to believe my story. It is not only true, nevertheless, but truth of which I have been an eyewitness.

It was a sweet summer evening, and my father asked me, as he sometimes did, to take a little ramble with him along that beautiful forest vista which I have mentioned as lying in front of the schloss.

'General Spielsdorf cannot come to us so soon as I had hoped,' said my father, as we pursued our walk.

He was to have paid us a visit of some weeks, and we had expected his arrival next day. He was to have brought with him a young lady, his niece and ward, Mademoiselle Rheinfeldt, whom I had never seen, but whom I had heard described as a very charming girl, and in whose society I had promised myself many happy days. I was more disappointed than a young lady living in a town, or a bustling neighbourhood can possibly imagine. This visit, and the new acquaintance it promised, had furnished my day dream for many weeks.

'And how soon does he come?' I asked.

'Not till autumn. Not for two months, I dare say,' he answered.

'And I am very glad now, dear, that you never knew Mademoiselle Rheinfeldt.'

'And why?' I asked, both mortified and curious.

'Because the poor young lady is dead,' he replied. 'I quite forgot I had not told you, but you were not in the room when I received the General's letter this evening.'

I was very much shocked. General Spielsdorf had mentioned in his first letter, six or seven weeks before, that she was not so well as he would wish her, but there was nothing to suggest the remotest suspicion of danger.

'Here is the General's letter,' he said, handing it to me. 'I am afraid he is in great affliction; the letter appears to me to have been written very nearly in distraction.'

We sat down on a rude bench, under a group of magnificent lime-trees. The sun was setting with all its melancholy splendour behind the sylvan horizon, and the stream that flows beside our home, and passes under the steep old bridge I have mentioned, wound through many a group of noble trees, almost at our feet, reflecting in its current the fading crimson of the sky. General Spielsdorf's letter was so extraordinary, so vehement, and in some places so self-contradictory, that I read it twice over—the second time aloud to my father—and was still unable to account for it, except by supposing that grief had unsettled his mind.

It said 'I have lost my darling daughter, for as such I loved her. During the last days of dear Bertha's illness I was not able to write to you. Before then I had no idea of her danger. I have lost her, and now learn *all*, too late. She died in the peace of innocence, and in the glorious hope of a blessed futurity. The fiend who betrayed our infatuated hospitality has done it all. I thought I was receiving into my house innocence, gaiety, a charming companion for my lost Bertha. Heavens! what a fool have I been! I thank God my child died without a suspicion of the

cause of her sufferings. She is gone without so much as conjec-
turing the nature of her illness, and the accursed passion of the
agent of all this misery. I devote my remaining days to tracking
and extinguishing a monster. I am told I may hope to accomplish my righteous and merciful purpose. At present there is
scarcely a gleam of light to guide me. I curse my conceited incre-
dulity, my despicable affectation of superiority, my blindness,
my obstinacy—all—too late. I cannot write or talk collectedly
now. I am distracted. So soon as I shall have a little recovered, I
mean to devote myself for a time to enquiry, which may possibly
lead me as far as Vienna. Some time in the autumn, two months
hence, or earlier if I live, I will see you—that is, if you permit
me; I will then tell you all that I scarce dare put upon paper now.
Farewell. Pray for me, dear friend.'

In these terms ended this strange letter. Though I had never
seen Bertha Rheinfeldt my eyes filled with tears at the sudden
intelligence; I was startled, as well as profoundly disappointed.

The sun had now set, and it was twilight by the time I had
returned the General's letter to my father.

It was a soft[1] clear evening, and we loitered, speculating upon
the possible meanings of the violent and incoherent sentences
which I had just been reading. We had nearly a mile to walk before reaching the road that passes the schloss in front, and by
that time the moon was shining brilliantly. At the drawbridge
we met Madame Perrodon and Mademoiselle De Lafontaine,
who had come out, without their bonnets, to enjoy the exquisite moonlight.

We heard their voices gabbling in animated dialogue as we
approached. We joined them at the drawbridge, and turned
about to admire with them the beautiful scene.

The glade through which we had just walked lay before us. At
our left the narrow road wound away under clumps of lordly

trees, and was lost to sight amid the thickening forest. At the right the same road crosses the steep and picturesque bridge, near which stands a ruined tower which once guarded that pass; and beyond the bridge an abrupt eminence rises, covered with trees, and showing in the shadows some grey ivy-clustered rocks.

Over the sward and low grounds a thin film of mist was stealing, like smoke, marking the distances with a transparent veil; and here and there we could see the river faintly flashing in the moonlight.

No softer, sweeter scene could be imagined. The news I had just heard made it melancholy; but nothing could disturb its character of profound serenity, and the enchanted glory and vagueness of the prospect.

My father, who enjoyed the picturesque, and I, stood looking in silence over the expanse beneath us. The two good governesses, standing a little way behind us, discoursed upon the scene, and were eloquent upon the moon.

Madame Perrodon was fat, middle-aged, and romantic, and talked and sighed poetically. Mademoiselle De Lafontaine—in right of her father, who was a German, assumed to be psychological, metaphysical, and something of a mystic—now declared that when the moon shone with a light so intense it was well known that it indicated a special spiritual activity. The effect of the full moon in such a state of brilliancy was manifold. It acted on dreams, it acted on lunacy, it acted on nervous people; it had marvellous physical influences connected with life. Mademoiselle related that her cousin, who was mate of a merchant ship, having taken a nap on deck on such a night, lying on his back, with his face full in the light on the moon, had wakened, after a dream of an old woman clawing him by the cheek, with his features horribly drawn to one side; and his countenance had never quite recovered its equilibrium.

'The moon, this night,' she said, 'is full of odylic[2] and magnetic influence—and see, when you look behind you at the front of the schloss, how all its windows flash and twinkle with that silvery splendour, as if unseen hands had lighted up the rooms to receive fairy guests.'

There are indolent states of the spirits in which, indisposed to talk ourselves, the talk of others is pleasant to our listless ears; and I gazed on, pleased with the tinkle of the ladies' conversation.

'I have got into one of my moping moods to-night,' said my father, after a silence, and quoting Shakespeare, whom, by way of keeping up our English, he used to read aloud, he said:

> ' "In truth I know not why I am so sad:
> It wearies me; you say it wearies you;
> But how I got it—came by it."[3]

'I forget the rest. But I feel as if some great misfortune were hanging over us. I suppose the poor General's afflicted letter has had something to do with it.'

At this moment the unwonted sound of carriage wheels and many hoofs upon the road, arrested our attention.

They seemed to be approaching from the high ground overlooking the bridge, and very soon the equipage emerged from that point. Two horsemen first crossed the bridge, then came a carriage drawn by four horses, and two men rode behind.

It seemed to be the travelling carriage of a person of rank; and we were all immediately absorbed in watching that very unusual spectacle. It became, in a few moments, greatly more interesting, for just as the carriage had passed the summit of the steep bridge, one of the leaders, taking fright, communicated his panic to the rest, and after a plunge[4] or two, the whole team

broke into a wild gallop together, and dashing between the
horsemen who rode in front, came thundering along the road
towards us with the speed of a hurricane.

The excitement of the scene was made more painful by the
clear, long-drawn screams of a female voice from the carriage
window.

We all advanced in curiosity and horror; my father in silence,
the rest with various ejaculations of terror.

Our suspense did not last long. Just before you reach the castle drawbridge, on the route they were coming, there stands by
the roadside a magnificent lime-tree, on the other stands an ancient stone cross, at sight of which the horses, now going at a
pace that was perfectly frightful, swerved so as to bring the
wheel over the projecting roots of the tree.

I knew what was coming. I covered my eyes, unable to see it
out, and turned my head away; at the same moment I heard a
cry from my lady-friends, who had gone on a little.

Curiosity opened my eyes, and I saw a scene of utter confusion. Two of the horses were on the ground, the carriage lay
upon its side with two wheels in the air; the men were busy removing the traces,[5] and a lady, with a commanding air and figure had got out, and stood with clasped hands, raising the
handkerchief that was in them every now and then to her eyes.
Through the carriage door was now lifted a young lady, who appeared to be lifeless. My dear old father was already beside the
elder lady, with his hat in his hand, evidently tendering his aid
and the resources of his schloss. The lady did not appear to hear
him, or to have eyes for anything but the slender girl who was
being placed against the slope of the bank.

I approached; the young lady was apparently stunned, but she
was certainly not dead. My father, who piqued himself on being
something of a physician, had just had his fingers to her wrist

and assured the lady, who declared herself her mother, that her pulse, though faint and irregular, was undoubtedly still distinguishable. The lady clasped her hands and looked upward, as if in a momentary transport of gratitude; but immediately she broke out again in that theatrical way which is, I believe, natural to some people.

She was what is called a fine looking woman for her time of life, and must have been handsome; she was tall, but not thin, and dressed in black velvet, and looked rather pale, but with a proud and commanding countenance, though now agitated strangely.

'Was ever being so born to calamity?' I heard her say, with clasped hands, as I came up. 'Here am I, on a journey of life and death, in prosecuting which to lose an hour is possibly to lose all. My child will not have recovered sufficiently to resume her route for who can say how long. I must leave her; I cannot, dare not, delay. How far on, sir, can you tell, is the nearest village? I must leave her there; and shall not see my darling, or even hear of her, till my return, three months hence.'

I plucked my father by the coat, and whispered earnestly in his ear: 'Oh! papa, pray ask her to let her stay with us—it would be so delightful. Do, pray.'

'If Madame will entrust her child to the care of my daughter, and of her good gouvernante, Madame Perrodon, and permit her to remain as our guest, under my charge, until her return, it will confer a distinction and an obligation upon us, and we shall treat her with all the care and devotion which so sacred a trust deserves.'

'I cannot do that, sir, it would be to task your kindness and chivalry too cruelly,' said the lady, distractedly.

'It would, on the contrary, be to confer on us a very great kindness at the moment when we most need it. My daughter has just been disappointed by a cruel misfortune, in a visit from which she had long anticipated a great deal of happiness. If you confide this young lady to our care it will be her best consolation. The nearest village on your route is distant, and affords no such inn as you could think of placing your daughter at; you cannot allow her to continue her journey for any considerable distance without danger. If, as you say, you cannot suspend your journey, you must part with her to-night, and nowhere could you do so with more honest assurances of care and tenderness than here.'

There was something in this lady's air and appearance so distinguished, and even imposing, and in her manner so engaging, as to impress one, quite apart from the dignity of her equipage, with a conviction that she was a person of consequence.

By this time the carriage was replaced in its upright position, and the horses, quite tractable, in the traces again.

The lady threw on her daughter a glance which I fancied was not quite so affectionate as one might have anticipated from the beginning of the scene; then she beckoned slightly to my father, and withdrew two or three steps with him out of hearing; and talked to him with a fixed and stern countenance, not at all like that with which she had hitherto spoken.

I was filled with wonder that my father did not seem to perceive the change, and also unspeakably curious to learn what it could be that she was speaking, almost in his ear, with so much earnestness and rapidity.

Two or three minutes at most I think she remained thus employed, then she turned, and a few steps brought her to where her daughter lay, supported by Madame Perrodon. She kneeled beside her for a moment and whispered, as Madame supposed, a little benediction in her ear; then hastily kissing her she stepped into her carriage, the door was closed, the footmen in stately liveries jumped up behind, the outriders spurred on, the postillions cracked their whips, the horses plunged and broke suddenly into a furious canter that threatened soon again to become a gallop, and the carriage whirled away, followed at the same rapid pace by the two horsemen in the rear.

CHAPTER III

We Compare Notes.

We followed the *cortège* with our eyes until it was swiftly lost to sight in the misty wood; and the very sound of the hoofs and the wheels died away in the silent night air.

Nothing remained to assure us that the adventure had not been an illusion of a moment but the young lady, who just at that moment opened her eyes. I could not see, for her face was turned from me, but she raised her head, evidently looking about her, and I heard a very sweet voice ask complainingly, 'Where is mamma?'

Our good Madame Perrodon answered tenderly, and added some comfortable assurances.

I then heard her ask:

'Where am I? What is this place?' and after that she said, 'I don't see the carriage; and Matska,[1] where is she?'

Madame answered all her questions in so far as she understood them; and gradually the young lady remembered how the misadventure came about, and was glad to hear that no one in, or in attendance on, the carriage was hurt; and on learning that her mamma had left her here, till her return in about three months, she wept.

I was going to add my consolations to those of Madame

Perrodon when Mademoiselle De Lafontaine placed her hand upon my arm, saying:

'Don't approach, one at a time is as much as she can at present converse with; a very little excitement would possibly overpower her now.'

As soon as she is comfortably in bed, I thought, I will run up to her room and see her.

My father in the meantime had sent a servant on horseback for the physician, who lived about two leagues away; and a bedroom was being prepared for the young lady's reception.

The stranger now rose, and leaning on Madame's arm, walked slowly over the drawbridge and into the castle gate.

In the hall, servants waited to receive her, and she was conducted forthwith to her room.

The room we usually sat in as our drawing room is long, having four windows, that looked over the moat and drawbridge, upon the forest scene I have just described.

It is furnished in old carved oak, with large carved cabinets, and the chairs are cushioned with crimson Utrecht velvet. The walls are covered with tapestry, and surrounded with great gold frames, the figures being as large as life, in ancient and very curious costume, and the subjects represented are hunting, hawking, and generally festive. It is not too stately to be extremely comfortable; and here we had our tea, for with his usual patriotic leanings he insisted that the national beverage should make its appearance regularly with our coffee and chocolate.

We sat here this night, and with candles lighted, were talking over the adventure of the evening.

Madame Perrodon and Mademoiselle De Lafontaine were both of our party. The young stranger had hardly lain down in her bed when she sank into a deep sleep; and those ladies had left her in the care of a servant.

'How do you like our guest?' I asked, as soon as Madame entered. 'Tell me all about her?'

'I like her extremely,' answered Madame, 'she is, I almost think, the prettiest creature I ever saw; about your age, and so gentle and nice.'

'She is absolutely beautiful,' threw in Mademoiselle, who had peeped for a moment into the stranger's room.

'And such a sweet voice!' added Madame Perrodon.

'Did you remark a woman in the carriage, after it was set up again, who did not get out,' inquired Mademoiselle, 'but only looked from the window?'

'No, we had not seen her.'

Then she described a hideous black woman, with a sort of coloured turban on her head, who was gazing all the time from the carriage window, nodding and grinning derisively towards the ladies, with gleaming eyes and large white eyeballs, and her teeth set as if in fury.

'Did you remark what an ill-looking pack of men the servants were?' asked Madame.

'Yes,' said my father, who had just come in, 'Ugly, hang-dog looking fellows, as ever I beheld in my life. I hope they mayn't rob the poor lady in the forest. They are clever rogues, however; they got everything to rights in a minute.'

'I dare say they are worn out with too long travelling,' said Madame. 'Besides looking wicked, their faces were so strangely lean, and dark, and sullen. I am very curious, I own; but I dare say the young lady will tell us all about it to-morrow, if she is sufficiently recovered.'

'I don't think she will,' said my father, with a mysterious smile, and a little nod of his head, as if he knew more about it than he cared to tell us.

This made me all the more inquisitive as to what had passed

between him and the lady in the black velvet, in the brief but earnest interview that had immediately preceded her departure.

We were scarcely alone, when I entreated him to tell me. He did not need much pressing.

'There is no particular reason why I should not tell you. She expressed a reluctance to trouble us with the care of her daughter, saying she was in delicate health, and nervous, but not subject to any kind of seizure—she volunteered that—nor to any illusion; being, in fact, perfectly sane.'

'How very odd to say all that!' I interpolated. 'It was so unnecessary.'

'At all events it *was* said,' he laughed, 'and as you wish to know all that passed, which was indeed very little, I tell you. She then said, "I am making a long journey of *vital* importance—she emphasized the word—rapid and secret; I shall return for my child in three months; in the meantime, she will be silent as to who we are, whence we come, and whither we are travelling." That is all she said. She spoke very pure French. When she said the word "secret," she paused for a few seconds, looking sternly, her eyes fixed on mine. I fancy she makes a great point of that. You saw how quickly she was gone. I hope I have not done a very foolish thing, in taking charge of the young lady.'

For my part, I was delighted. I was longing to see and talk to her; and only waiting till the doctor should give me leave. You, who live in towns, can have no idea how great an event the introduction of a new friend is, in such a solitude as surrounded us.

The doctor did not arrive till nearly one o'clock; but I could no more have gone to my bed and slept, than I could have overtaken, on foot, the carriage in which the princess in black velvet had driven away.

When the physician came down to the drawing-room, it was to report very favourably upon his patient. She was now sitting up, her pulse quite regular, apparently perfectly well. She had sustained no injury, and the little shock to her nerves had passed away quite harmlessly. There could be no harm certainly in my seeing her, if we both wished it; and, with this permission, I sent, forthwith, to know whether she would allow me to visit her for a few minutes in her room.

The servant returned immediately to say that she desired nothing more.

You may be sure I was not long in availing myself of this permission.

Our visitor lay in one of the handsomest rooms in the schloss. It was, perhaps, a little stately. There was a sombre piece of tapestry opposite the foot of the bed, representing Cleopatra with the asps to her bosom;[2] and other solemn classic scenes were displayed, a little faded, upon the other walls. But there was gold carving, and rich and varied colour enough in the other decorations of the room, to more than redeem the gloom of the old tapestry.

There were candles at the bed side. She was sitting up; her slender pretty figure enveloped in the soft silk dressing gown, embroidered with flowers, and lined with thick quilted silk, which her mother had thrown over her feet as she lay upon the ground.

What was it that, as I reached the bed-side and had just begun my little greeting, struck me dumb in a moment, and made me recoil a step or two from before her? I will tell you.

I saw the very face which had visited me in my childhood at night, which remained so fixed in my memory, and on which I had for so many years so often ruminated with horror, when no one suspected of what I was thinking.

It was pretty, even beautiful; and when I first beheld it, wore the same melancholy expression.

But this almost instantly lighted into a strange fixed smile of recognition.

There was a silence of fully a minute, and then at length *she* spoke; *I* could not.

'How wonderful!' she exclaimed. 'Twelve years ago, I saw your face in a dream, and it has haunted me ever since.'

'Wonderful, indeed!' I repeated, overcoming with an effort the horror that had for a time suspended my utterances. 'Twelve years ago, in vision or reality, *I* certainly saw you. I could not forget your face. It has remained before my eyes ever since.'

Her smile had softened. Whatever I had fancied strange in it, was gone, and it and her dimpling cheeks were now delightfully pretty and intelligent.

I felt reassured, and continued more in the vein which hospitality indicated, to bid her welcome, and to tell her how much pleasure her accidental arrival had given us all, and especially what a happiness it was to me.

I took her hand as I spoke. I was a little shy, as lonely people are, but the situation made me eloquent, and even bold. She pressed my hand, she laid hers upon it, and her eyes glowed, as, looking hastily into mine, she smiled again, and blushed.

She answered my welcome very prettily. I sat down beside her, still wondering; and she said:

'I must tell you my vision about you; it is so very strange that you and I should have had, each of the other so vivid a dream, that each should have seen, I you and you me, looking as we do now, when of course we both were mere children. I was a child, about six years old, and I awoke from a confused and troubled dream, and found myself in a room, unlike my nursery, wainscoted clumsily in some dark wood, and with cupboards and bedsteads, and chairs, and benches placed about it. The beds were, I thought, all empty, and the room itself without anyone but myself in it; and I, after looking about me for some time, and admiring especially an iron candlestick, with two branches, which I should certainly know again, crept under one of the beds to reach the window; but as I got from under the bed, I heard someone crying; and looking up, while I was still upon my knees, I saw *you*—most assuredly you—as I see you now; a beautiful young lady, with golden hair and large blue eyes, and lips—your lips—you, as you are here. Your looks won me; I climbed on the bed and put my arms about you, and I think we both fell asleep. I was roused by a scream; you were sitting up screaming. I was frightened, and slipped down upon the ground, and, it seemed to me, lost consciousness for a moment; and when I came to myself, I was again in my nursery at home. Your face I have never forgotten since. I could not be misled by mere resemblance. You *are* the lady whom I then saw.'

It was now my turn to relate my corresponding vision, which I did, to the undisguised wonder of my new acquaintance.

'I don't know which should be most afraid of the other,' she said, again smiling—'If you were less pretty I think I should be very much afraid of you, but being as you are, and you and I both so young, I feel only that I have made your acquaintance twelve years ago, and have already a right to your intimacy; at all events it does seem as if we were destined, from our earliest childhood, to be friends. I wonder whether you feel as strangely drawn towards me as I do to you; I have never had a friend— shall I find one now?' She sighed, and her fine dark eyes gazed passionately on me.

Now the truth is, I felt rather unaccountably towards the beautiful stranger. I did feel, as she said, 'drawn towards her,' but there was also something of repulsion. In this ambiguous feeling, however, the sense of attraction immensely prevailed. She interested and won me; she was so beautiful and so indescribably engaging.

I perceived now something of languor and exhaustion stealing over her, and hastened to bid her good night.

'The doctor thinks,' I added, 'that you ought to have a maid to sit up with you to-night; one of ours is waiting, and you will find her a very useful and quiet creature.'

'How kind of you, but I could not sleep, I never could with an attendant in the room. I shan't require any assistance—and, shall I confess my weakness, I am haunted with a terror of robbers. Our house was robbed once, and two servants murdered, so I always lock my door. It has become a habit—and you look so kind I know you will forgive me. I see there is a key in the lock.'

She held me close in her pretty arms for a moment and whispered in my ear, 'Good night, darling, it is very hard to part with you, but good night; to-morrow, but not early, I shall see you again.'

She sank back on the pillow with a sigh, and her fine eyes followed me with a fond and melancholy gaze, and she murmured again 'Good night, dear friend.'

Young people like, and even love, on impulse. I was flattered by the evident, though as yet undeserved, fondness she showed me. I liked the confidence with which she at once received me. She was determined that we should be very near friends.

Next day came and we met again. I was delighted with my companion; that is to say, in many respects.

Her looks lost nothing in daylight—she was certainly the most beautiful creature I had ever seen, and the unpleasant remembrance of the face presented in my early dream, had lost the effect of the first unexpected recognition.

She confessed that she had experienced a similar shock on seeing me, and precisely the same faint antipathy that had mingled with my admiration of her. We now laughed together over our momentary horrors.

CHAPTER IV

Her Habits—A Saunter.

I told you that I was charmed with her in most particulars.

There were some that did not please me so well.

She was above the middle height of women. I shall begin by describing her. She was slender, and wonderfully graceful. Except that her movements were languid—*very* languid—indeed, there was nothing in her appearance to indicate an invalid. Her complexion was rich and brilliant; her features were small and beautifully formed; her eyes large, dark, and lustrous; her hair was quite wonderful, I never saw hair so magnificently thick and long when it was down about her shoulders; I have often placed my hands under it, and laughed with wonder at its weight. It was exquisitely fine and soft, and in colour a rich very dark brown, with something of gold. I loved to let it down, tumbling with its own weight, as, in her room, she lay back in her chair talking in her sweet low voice, I used to fold and braid it, and spread it out and play with it. Heavens! If I had but known all!

I said there were particulars which did not please me. I have told you that her confidence won me the first night I saw her; but I found that she exercised with respect to herself, her mother, her history, everything in fact connected with her life, plans, and people, an ever wakeful reserve. I dare say I was unreasonable, perhaps I was wrong; I dare say I ought to have respected the solemn injunction laid upon my father by the stately lady in black velvet. But curiosity is a restless and unscrupulous passion, and no one girl can endure, with patience, that hers should be baffled by another. What harm could it do anyone to tell me what I so ardently desired to know? Had she no trust in my good sense or honour? Why would she not believe me when I assured her, so solemnly, that I would not divulge one syllable of what she told me to any mortal breathing.

There was a coldness, it seemed to me, beyond her years, in her smiling melancholy persistent refusal to afford me the least ray of light.

I cannot say we quarreled upon this point, for she would not quarrel upon any. It was, of course, very unfair of me to press her, very ill-bred, but I really could not help it; and I might just as well have let it alone.

What she did tell me amounted, in my unconscionable estimation—to nothing.

It was all summed up in three very vague disclosures:

First.—Her name was Carmilla.

Second.—Her family was very ancient and noble.

Third.—Her home lay in the direction of the west.

She would not tell me the name of her family, nor their armorial bearings,[1] nor the name of their estate, nor even that of the country they lived in.

You are not to suppose that I worried her incessantly on these subjects. I watched opportunity, and rather insinuated than urged my inquiries. Once or twice, indeed, I did attack her more directly. But no matter what my tactics, utter failure was invariably the result. Reproaches and caresses were all lost upon her. But I must add this, that her evasion was conducted with so pretty a melancholy and deprecation, with so many, and even passionate declarations of her liking for me, and trust in my honour, and with so many promises that I should at last know all, that I could not find it in my heart long to be offended with her.

She used to place her pretty arms about my neck, draw me to her, and laying her cheek to mine, murmur with her lips near my ear, 'Dearest, your little heart is wounded; think me not cruel because I obey the irresistible law of my strength and weakness; if your dear heart is wounded, my wild heart bleeds with yours. In the rapture of my enormous humiliation I live in your warm life, and you shall die—die, sweetly die—into mine. I cannot help it; as I draw near to you, you, in your turn, will draw near to others, and learn the rapture of that cruelty, which yet is love; so, for a while, seek to know no more of me and mine, but trust me with all your loving spirit.'

And when she had spoken such a rhapsody, she would press me more closely in her trembling embrace, and her lips in soft kisses gently glow upon my cheek.

Her agitations and her language were unintelligible to me.

From these foolish embraces, which were not of very frequent occurrence, I must allow, I used to wish to extricate myself; but my energies seemed to fail me. Her murmured words sounded like a lullaby in my ear, and soothed my resistance into a trance, from which I only seemed to recover myself when she withdrew her arms.

In these mysterious moods I did not like her. I experienced a strange tumultuous excitement that was pleasurable, ever and anon, mingled with a vague sense of fear and disgust. I had no distinct thoughts about her while such scenes lasted, but I was conscious of a love growing into adoration, and also of abhorrence. This I know is paradox, but I can make no other attempt to explain the feeling.

I now write, after an interval of more than ten years, with a trembling hand, with a confused and horrible recollection of certain occurrences and situations, in the ordeal through which I was unconsciously passing; though with a vivid and very sharp remembrance of the main current of my story. But, I suspect, in all lives there are certain emotional scenes, those in which our passions have been most wildly and terribly roused, that are of all others the most vaguely and dimly remembered.

Sometimes after an hour of apathy, my strange and beautiful companion would take my hand and hold it with a fond pressure, renewed again and again; blushing softly, gazing in my face with languid and burning eyes, and breathing so fast that her dress rose and fell with the tumultuous respiration. It was like the ardour of a lover; it embarrassed me; it was hateful and yet over-powering; and with gloating eyes she drew me to her, and her hot lips travelled along my cheek in kisses; and she would whisper, almost in sobs, 'You are mine, you *shall* be mine, you and I are one for ever.' Then she has thrown herself back in her chair, with her small hands over her eyes, leaving me trembling.

'Are we related,' I used to ask; 'what can you mean by all this? I remind you perhaps of some one whom you love; but you must not, I hate it; I don't know you—I don't know myself when you look so and talk so.'

She used to sigh at my vehemence, then turn away and drop my hand.

Respecting these very extraordinary manifestations I strove in vain to form any satisfactory theory—I could not refer them to affectation or trick. It was unmistakably the momentary breaking out of suppressed instinct and emotion. Was she, notwithstanding her mother's volunteered denial, subject to brief visitations of insanity; or was there here a disguise and a romance? I had read in old story books of such things. What if a boyish lover had found his way into the house, and sought to prosecute his suit in masquerade, with the assistance of a clever old adventuress. But there were many things against this hypothesis, highly interesting as it was to my vanity.

I could boast of no little attentions such as masculine gallantry delights to offer. Between these passionate moments there were long intervals of common-place, of gaiety, of brooding melancholy, during which, except that I detected her eyes so full of melancholy fire, following me, at times I might have been as nothing to her. Except in these brief periods of mysterious excitement her ways were girlish; and there was always a languor about her, quite incompatible with a masculine system in a state of health.

In some respects her habits were odd. Perhaps not so singular in the opinion of a town lady like you, as they appeared to us rustic people. She used to come down very late, generally not till one o'clock, she would then take a cup of chocolate, but eat nothing; we then went out for a walk, which was a mere saunter, and she seemed, almost immediately, exhausted, and either returned to the schloss or sat on one of the benches that were placed, here and there, among the trees. This was a bodily languor in which her mind did not sympathise. She was always an animated talker, and very intelligent.

She sometimes alluded for a moment to her own home, or mentioned an adventure or situation, or an early recollection, which indicated a people of strange manners, and described customs of which we knew nothing. I gathered from these chance hints that her native country was much more remote than I had at first fancied.

As we sat thus one afternoon under the trees a funeral passed us by. It was that of a pretty young girl, whom I had often seen,

the daughter of one of the rangers of the forest. The poor man
was walking behind the coffin of his darling; she was his only
child, and he looked quite heartbroken. Peasants walking two-
and-two came behind, they were singing a funeral hymn.

I rose to mark my respect as they passed, and joined in the
hymn they were very sweetly singing.

My companion shook me a little roughly, and I turned surprised.

She said brusquely, 'Don't you perceive how discordant that is?'

'I think it very sweet, on the contrary,' I answered, vexed at
the interruption, and very uncomfortable, lest the people who
composed the little procession should observe and resent what
was passing.

I resumed, therefore, instantly, and was again interrupted.
'You pierce my ears,' said Carmilla, almost angrily, and stop-
ping her ears with her tiny fingers. 'Besides, how can you tell
that your religion and mine are the same; your forms wound me,
and I hate funerals. What a fuss! Why *you* must die—*everyone*
must die; and all are happier when they do. Come home.'

'My father has gone on with the clergyman to the churchyard. I thought you knew she was to be buried to day.'

'*She?* I don't trouble my head about peasants. I don't know
who she is,' answered Carmilla, with a flash from her fine eyes.

'She is the poor girl who fancied she saw a ghost a fortnight
ago, and has been dying ever since, till yesterday, when she ex-
pired.'

'Tell me nothing about ghosts. I shan't sleep to-night if you do.'

'I hope there is no plague or fever coming; all this looks very
like it,' I continued. 'The swineherd's young wife died only a
week ago, and she thought something seized her by the throat as
she lay in her bed, and nearly strangled her. Papa says such horrible fancies do accompany some forms of fever. She was quite

well the day before. She sank afterwards, and died before a week.'

'Well, *her* funeral is over, I hope, and *her* hymn sung; and our ears shan't be tortured with that discord and jargon.[2] It has made me nervous. Sit down here, beside me; sit close; hold my hand; press it hard—hard—harder.'

We had moved a little back, and had come to another seat.

She sat down. Her face underwent a change that alarmed and even terrified me for a moment. It darkened, and became horribly livid; her teeth and hands were clenched, and she frowned and compressed her lips, while she stared down upon the ground at her feet, and trembled all over with a continued shudder as irrepressible as ague.[3] All her energies seemed strained to suppress a fit, with which she was then breathlessly tugging; and at length a low convulsive cry of suffering broke from her, and gradually the hysteria subsided. 'There! That comes of strangling people with hymns!' she said at last. 'Hold me, hold me still. It is passing away.'

And so gradually it did; and perhaps to dissipate the somber impression which the spectacle had left upon me, she became unusually animated and chatty; and so we got home.

This was the first time I had seen her exhibit any definable symptoms of that delicacy of health which her mother had spoken of. It was the first time, also, I had seen her exhibit anything like temper.

Both passed away like a summer cloud; and never but once afterwards did I witness on her part a momentary sign of anger. I will tell you how it happened.

She and I were looking out of one of the long drawing-room windows, when there entered the court-yard, over the draw-bridge, a figure of a wanderer whom I knew very well. He used to visit the schloss generally twice a year.

It was the figure of a hunchback, with the sharp lean features that generally accompany deformity. He wore a pointed black beard, and he was smiling from ear to ear, showing his white fangs. He was dressed in buff, black, and scarlet, and crossed with more straps and belts than I could count, from which hung all manner of things. Behind, he carried a magic-lantern,[4] and two boxes, which I well knew, in one of which was a salamander, and in the other a mandrake.[5] These monsters used to make my father laugh. They were compounded of parts of monkeys, parrots, squirrels, fish, and hedgehogs, dried and stitched together with great neatness and startling effect. He had a fiddle, a box of conjuring apparatus, a pair of foils and masks[6] attached to his belt, several other mysterious cases dangling about him, and a black staff with copper ferrules in his hand. His companion was a rough spare dog, that followed at his heels, but stopped short, suspiciously at the drawbridge, and in a little while began to howl dismally.

In the meantime, the mountebank, standing in the midst of the court-yard, raised his grotesque hat, and made us a very ceremonious bow, paying his compliments very volubly in execrable French, and German not much better. Then, disengaging his fiddle, he began to scrape a lively air, to which he sang with a merry discord, dancing with ludicrous airs and activity, that made me laugh, in spite of the dog's howling.

Then he advanced to the window with many smiles and salutations, and his hat in his left hand, his fiddle under his arm, and with a fluency that never took breath, he gabbled a long advertisement of all his accomplishments, and the resources of the various arts which he placed at our service, and the curiosities and entertainments which it was in his power, at our bidding, to display.

'Will your ladyships be pleased to buy an amulet[7] against the oupire,[8] which is going like the wolf, I hear, through these woods,' he said, dropping his hat on the pavement. 'They are dying of it right and left, and here is a charm that never fails; only pinned to the pillow, and you may laugh in his face.'

These charms consisted of oblong slips of vellum, with cabalistic ciphers and diagrams upon them.

Carmilla instantly purchased one, and so did I.

He was looking up, and we were smiling down upon him, amused; at least, I can answer for myself. His piercing black eye, as he looked up in our faces, seemed to detect something that fixed for a moment his curiosity.

In an instant he unrolled a leather case, full of all manner of odd little steel instruments.

'See here, my lady,' he said, displaying it, and addressing me, 'I profess, among other things less useful, the art of dentistry. Plague take the dog!' he interpolated. 'Silence, beast! He howls so that your ladyships can scarcely hear a word. Your noble friend, the young lady at your right, has the sharpest tooth,— long, thin, pointed, like an awl, like a needle; ha, ha! With my sharp and long sight, as I look up, I have seen it distinctly; now if it happens to hurt the young lady, and I think it must, here am I, here are my file, my punch, my nippers; I will make it round and blunt, if her ladyship pleases; no longer the tooth of a fish, but of a beautiful young lady as she is. Hey? Is the young lady displeased? Have I been too bold? Have I offended her?'

The young lady, indeed, looked very angry as she drew back from the window.

'How dares that mountebank insult us so? Where is your father? I shall demand redress from him. My father would have had the wretch tied up to the pump, and flogged with a cartwhip, and burnt to the bones with the castle brand!'

She retired from the window a step or two, and sat down,

and had hardly lost sight of the offender, when her wrath subsided as suddenly as it had risen, and she gradually recovered
her usual tone, and seemed to forget the little hunchback and his
follies.

My father was out of spirits that evening. On coming in he
told us that there had been another case very similar to the two
fatal ones which had lately occurred. The sister of a young peasant on his estate, only a mile away, was very ill, had been, as she
described it, attacked very nearly in the same way, and was now
slowly but steadily sinking.

'All this,' said my father, 'is strictly referable to natural
causes. These poor people infect one another with their superstitions, and so repeat in imagination the images of terror that
have infested their neighbours.'

'But that very circumstance frightens one horribly,' said Carmilla.

'How so?' inquired my father.

'I am so afraid of fancying I see such things; I think it would
be as bad as reality.'

'We are in God's hands; nothing can happen without his permission, and all will end well for those who love him. He is our
faithful creator; He has made us all, and will take care of us.'

'Creator! *Nature!*' said the young lady in answer to my gentle
father. 'And this disease that invades the country is natural. Nature. All things proceed from Nature—don't they? All things in
the heaven, in the earth, and under the earth, act and live as Nature ordains? I think so.'

'The doctor said he would come here to-day,' said my father,
after a silence. 'I want to know what he thinks about it, and
what he thinks we had better do.'

'Doctors never did me any good,' said Carmilla.

'Then you have been ill?' I asked.

'More ill than ever you were,' she answered.

'Long ago?'

'Yes, a long time. I suffered from this very illness; but I forget all but my pain and weakness, and they were not so bad as are suffered in other diseases.'

'You were very young then?'

'I dare say; let us talk no more of it. You would not wound a friend?' She looked languidly in my eyes, and passed her arm round my waist lovingly, and led me out of the room. My father was busy over some papers near the window.

'Why does your papa like to frighten us?' said the pretty girl, with a sigh and a little shudder.

'He doesn't, dear Carmilla, it is the very furthest thing from his mind.'

'Are you afraid, dearest?'

'I should be very much if I fancied there was any real danger of my being attacked as those poor people were.'

'You are afraid to die?'

'Yes, every one is.'

'But to die as lovers may—to die together, so that they may live together. Girls are caterpillars while they live in the world, to be finally butterflies when the summer comes; but in the meantime there are grubs and larvæ, don't you see—each with their peculiar propensities, necessities, and structure. So says Monsieur Buffon,[9] in his big book, in the next room.'

Later in the day the doctor came, and was closeted with papa for some time. He was a skilful man, of sixty and upwards, he wore powder, and shaved his pale face as smooth as a pumpkin. He and papa emerged from the room together, and I heard papa laugh, and say as they came out:

'Well, I do wonder at a wise man like you. What do you say to hippogriffs[10] and dragons?'

The doctor was smiling, and made answer, shaking his head—

'Nevertheless life and death are mysterious states, and we know little of the resources of either.'

And so they walked on, and I heard no more. I did not then know what the doctor had been broaching, but I think I guess it now.

CHAPTER V

A Wonderful Likeness.

This evening there arrived from Gratz[1] the grave, dark-faced son of the picture cleaner, with a horse and cart laden with two large packing cases, having many pictures in each. It was a journey of ten leagues, and whenever a messenger arrived at the schloss from our little capital of Gratz, we used to crowd about him in the hall, to hear the news.

This arrival created in our secluded quarters quite a sensation. The cases remained in the hall, and the messenger was taken charge of by the servants till he had eaten his supper. Then with assistants, and armed with hammer, ripping-chisel, and turnscrew, he met us in the hall, where we had assembled to witness the unpacking of the cases.

Carmilla sat looking listlessly on, while one after the other the old pictures, nearly all portraits, which had undergone the process of renovation, were brought to light. My mother was of an old Hungarian family, and most of these pictures, which were about to be restored to their places, had come to us through her.

My father had a list in his hand, from which he read, as the artist rummaged out the corresponding numbers. I don't know that the pictures were very good, but they were, undoubtedly, very old, and some of them very curious also. They had, for the most part, the merit of being now seen by me, I may say, for the first time; for the smoke and dust of time had all but obliterated them.

'There is a picture that I have not seen yet,' said my father. 'In one corner, at the top of it, is the name, as well as I could read, "Marcia Karnstein," and the date "1698;" and I am curious to see how it has turned out.'

I remembered it; it was a small picture, about a foot and a half high, and nearly square, without a frame; but it was so blackened by age that I could not make it out.

The artist now produced it, with evident pride. It was quite beautiful; it was startling; it seemed to live. It was the effigy[2] of Carmilla!

'Carmilla, dear, here is an absolute miracle. Here you are, living, smiling, ready to speak, in this picture. Isn't it beautiful, papa? And see, even the little mole on her throat.'

My father laughed, and said 'Certainly it is a wonderful likeness,' but he looked away, and to my surprise seemed but little struck by it, and went on talking to the picture cleaner, who was also something of an artist, and discoursed with intelligence about the portraits or other works, which his art had just brought into light and colour, while I was more and more lost in wonder the more I looked at the picture.

'Will you let me hang this picture in my room, papa?' I asked.

'Certainly, dear,' said he, smiling, 'I'm very glad you think it so like. It must be prettier even than I thought it, if it is.'

The young lady did not acknowledge this pretty speech, did not seem to hear it. She was leaning back in her seat, her fine eyes under their long lashes gazing on me in contemplation, and she smiled in a kind of rapture.

'And now you can read quite plainly the name that is written in the corner. It is not Marcia; it looks as if it was done in gold. The name is Mircalla, Countess Karnstein, and this is a little coronet over it, and underneath A.D. 1698. I am descended from the Karnsteins; that is, mamma was.'

'Ah!' said the lady, languidly, 'so am I, I think, a very long descent, very ancient. Are there any Karnsteins living now?'

'None who bear the name, I believe. The family were ruined, I believe, in some civil wars, long ago, but the ruins of the castle are only about three miles away.'

'How interesting!' she said, languidly. 'But see what beautiful moonlight!' She glanced through the hall-door, which stood a little open. 'Suppose you take a little ramble round the court, and look down at the road and river.'

'It is so like the night you came to us,' I said.

She sighed, smiling.

She rose, and each with her arm about the other's waist, we walked out upon the pavement.

In silence, slowly we walked down to the drawbridge, where the beautiful landscape opened before us.

'And so you were thinking of the night I came here?' she almost whispered. 'Are you glad I came?'

'Delighted, dear Carmilla,' I answered.

'And you asked for the picture you think like me, to hang in your room,' she murmured with a sigh, as she drew her arm closer about my waist, and let her pretty head sink upon my shoulder.

'How romantic you are, Carmilla,' I said. 'Whenever you tell me your story, it will be made up chiefly of some one great romance.'[3]

She kissed me silently.

'I am sure, Carmilla, you have been in love; that there is, at this moment, an affair of the heart going on.'

'I have been in love with no one, and never shall,' she whispered, 'Unless it should be with you.'

How beautiful she looked in the moonlight!

Shy and strange was the look with which she quickly hid her face in my neck and hair, with tumultuous sighs, that seemed almost to sob, and pressed in mine a hand that trembled.

Her soft cheek was glowing against mine. 'Darling, darling,' she murmured, 'I live in you; and you would die for me, I love you so.'

I started from her.

She was gazing on me with eyes from which all fire, all meaning had flown, and a face colorless and apathetic.

'Is there a chill in the air, dear?' she said drowsily. 'I almost shiver; have I been dreaming? Let us come in. Come; come; come in.'

'You look ill, Carmilla; a little faint. You must take some wine,' I said.

'Yes. I will. I'm better now. I shall be quite well in a few minutes. Yes, do give me a little wine,' answered Carmilla, as we approached the door. 'Let us look again for a moment; it is the last time, perhaps, I shall see the moonlight with you.'

'How do you feel now, dear Carmilla? Are you really better?' I asked.

I was beginning to take alarm, lest she should have been stricken with the strange epidemic that they said had invaded the country about us.

'Papa would be grieved beyond measure,' I added, 'if he thought you were ever so little ill, without immediately letting us know. We have a very skilful doctor near us, the physician who was with papa to-day.'

'I'm sure he is. I know how kind you all are; but, dear child, I am quite well again. There is nothing ever wrong with me, but a little weakness. People say I am languid; I am incapable of exertion; I can scarcely walk as far as a child of three years old; and every now and then the little strength I have falters, and I become as you have just seen me. But after all I am very easily set up again; in a moment I am perfectly myself. See how I have recovered.'

So, indeed, she had; and she and I talked a great deal, and very animated she was; and the remainder of that evening passed without any recurrence of what I called her infatuations. I mean her crazy talk and looks, which embarrassed, and even frightened me.

But there occurred that night an event which gave my thoughts quite a new turn, and seemed to startle even Carmilla's languid nature into momentary energy.

CHAPTER VI.

A Very Strange Agony.

When we got into the drawing-room, and had sat down to our coffee and chocolate, although Carmilla did not take any, she seemed quite herself again, and Madame, and Mademoiselle De Lafontaine, joined us, and made a little card party, in the course of which papa came in for what he called his 'dish of tea.'[1]

When the game was over he sat down beside Carmilla on the sofa, and asked her, a little anxiously, whether she had heard from her mother since her arrival.

She answered 'No.'

He then asked whether she knew where a letter would reach her at present.

'I cannot tell,' she answered ambiguously, 'but I have been thinking of leaving you; you have been already too hospitable and too kind to me. I have given you an infinity of trouble, and I should wish to take a carriage to-morrow, and post[2] in pursuit of her; I know where I shall ultimately find her, although I dare not yet tell you.'

'But you must not dream of any such thing,' exclaimed my father, to my great relief. 'We can't afford to lose you so, and I won't consent to your leaving us, except under the care of your mother, who was so good as to consent to your remaining with us till she should herself return. I should be quite happy if I knew that you heard from her; but this evening the accounts of the progress of the mysterious disease that has invaded our neighborhood, grow even more alarming; and my beautiful guest, I do feel the responsibility, unaided by advice from your mother, very much. But I shall do my best; and one thing is certain, that you must not think of leaving us without her distinct direction to that effect. We should suffer too much in parting from you to consent to it easily.'

'Thank you, sir, a thousand times for your hospitality,' she answered, smiling bashfully. 'You have all been too kind to me; I have seldom been so happy in all my life before, as in your beautiful château, under your care, and in the society of your dear daughter.'

So he gallantly, in his old-fashioned way, kissed her hand, smiling and pleased at her little speech.

I accompanied Carmilla as usual to her room, and sat and chatted with her while she was preparing for bed.

'Do you think,' I said at length, 'that you will ever confide fully in me?'

She turned round smiling, but made no answer, only continued to smile on me.

'You won't answer that?' I said. 'You can't answer pleasantly; perhaps I ought not to have asked you.'

'You were quite right to ask me that, or anything. You do not know how dear you are to me, or you could not think any confidence too great to look for. But I am under vows, no nun half so awfully, and I dare not tell my story yet, even to you. The time is very near when you shall know everything. You will think me cruel, very selfish, but love is always selfish; the more ardent the more selfish. How jealous I am you cannot know. You must come with me, loving me, to death; or else hate me and still come with me, and *hating* me through death and after. There is no such word as indifference in my apathetic nature.'

'Now, Carmilla, you are going to talk your wild nonsense again,' I said hastily.

'Not I, silly little fool as I am, and full of whims and fancies; for your sake I'll talk like a sage. Were you ever at a ball?'

'No; how you do run on. What is it like? How charming it must be.'

'I almost forget, it is years ago.'

I laughed.

'You are not so old. Your first ball can hardly be forgotten yet.'

'I remember everything about it—with an effort. I see it all, as divers see what is going on above them, through a medium, dense, rippling, but transparent. There occurred that night what has confused the picture, and made its colours faint. I was all but assassinated in my bed, wounded *here*,' she touched her breast, 'and never was the same since.'

'Were you near dying?'

'Yes, very—a cruel love—strange love, that would have taken my life. Love will have its sacrifices. No sacrifice without blood. Let us go to sleep now; I feel so lazy. How can I get up just now and lock my door?'

She was lying with her tiny hands buried in her rich wavy hair, under her cheek, her little head upon the pillow, and her glittering eyes followed me wherever I moved, with a kind of shy smile that I could not decipher.

I bid her good night, and crept from the room with an uncomfortable sensation.

I often wondered whether our pretty guest ever said her prayers. *I* certainly had never seen her upon her knees. In the morning she never came down until long after our family

prayers were over, and at night she never left the drawing-room
to attend our brief evening prayers in the hall.

If it had not been that it had casually come out in one of our
careless talks that she had been baptised, I should have doubted
her being a Christian. Religion was a subject on which I had
never heard her speak a word. If I had known the world better,
this particular neglect or antipathy would not have so much surprised me.

The precautions of nervous people are infectious, and persons
of a like temperament are pretty sure, after a time, to imitate
them. I had adopted Carmilla's habit of locking her bed-room
door, having taken into my head all her whimsical alarms about
midnight invaders and prowling assassins. I had also adopted
her precaution of making a brief search through her room, to
satisfy herself that no lurking assassin or robber was 'ensconced.'

These wise measures taken, I got into my bed and fell asleep.
A light was burning in my room. This was an old habit, of very
early date, and which nothing could have tempted me to dis-
pense with.

Thus fortified I might take my rest in peace. But dreams come
through stone walls, light up dark rooms, or darken light ones,
and their persons make their exits and their entrances as they
please, and laugh at locksmiths.

I had a dream that night that was the beginning of a very
strange agony.

I cannot call it a nightmare, for I was quite conscious of being
asleep. But I was equally conscious of being in my room, and
lying in bed, precisely as I actually was. I saw, or fancied I saw,
the room and its furniture just as I had seen it last, except that it
was very dark, and I saw something moving round the foot of
the bed, which at first I could not accurately distinguish. But I
soon saw that it was a sooty-black animal that resembled a

monstrous cat. It appeared to me about four or five feet long, for it measured fully the length of the hearth-rug as it passed over it; and it continued toing and froing with the lithe sinister rest-lessness of a beast in a cage. I could not cry out, although as you may suppose, I was terrified. Its pace was growing faster, and the room rapidly darker and darker, and at length so dark that I could no longer see anything of it but its eyes. I felt it spring lightly on the bed. The two broad eyes approached my face, and suddenly I felt a stinging pain as if two large needles darted, an inch or two apart, deep into my breast. I waked with a scream. The room was lighted by the candle that burnt there all through the night, and I saw a female figure standing at the foot of the bed, a little at the right side. It was in a dark loose dress, and its hair was down and covered its shoulders. A block of stone could not have been more still. There was not the slightest stir of res-piration. As I stared at it the figure appeared to have changed its place, and was now nearer the door; then, close to it, the door opened, and it passed out.

I was now relieved, and able to breathe and move. My first thought was that Carmilla had been playing me a trick, and that I had forgotten to secure my door. I hastened to it, and found it locked as usual on the inside. I was afraid to open it—I was hor-rified. I sprang into my bed and covered my head up in the bed-clothes, and lay there more dead than alive till morning.

CHAPTER VII.

Descending.

It would be vain my attempting to tell you the horror with which, even now, I recall the occurrence of that night. It was no such transitory terror as a dream leaves behind it. It seemed to deepen by time, and communicated itself to the room and the very furniture that had encompassed the apparition.

I could not bear next day to be alone for a moment. I should have told papa, but for two opposite reasons. At one time I thought he would laugh at my story, and I could not bear its being treated as a jest; and at another I thought he might fancy that I had been attacked by the mysterious complaint which had invaded our neighbourhood. I had myself no misgivings of the kind, and as he had been rather an invalid for some time, I was afraid of alarming him.

I was comfortable enough with my good-natured companions, Madame Paradon, and the vivacious Mademoiselle de Lafontaine.[1] They both perceived that I was out of spirits and nervous, and at length I told them what lay so heavy at my heart.

Mademoiselle laughed, but I fancied that Madame Paradon looked anxious.

'By-the-by,' said Mademoiselle, laughing, 'the long lime-tree walk, behind Carmilla's bedroom-window, is haunted!'

'Nonsense!' exclaimed Madame, who probably thought the theme rather inopportune, 'and who tells that story, my dear?'

'Martin says that he came up twice, when the old yard-gate was being repaired, before sunrise, and twice saw the same female figure walking down the lime-tree avenue.'

'So he well might, as long as there are cows to milk in the river fields,' said Madame.

'I daresay; but Martin chooses to be frightened, and never did I see fool[2] *more* frightened.'

'You must not say a word about it to Carmilla, because she can see down that walk from her room window,' I interposed, 'and she is, if possible, a greater coward than I.'

Carmilla came down rather later than usual that day.

'I was so frightened last night,' she said, so soon as [we] were together, 'and I am sure I should have seen something dreadful if it had not been for that charm I bought from the poor little hunchback whom I called such hard names. I had a dream of something black coming round my bed, and I awoke in a perfect horror, and I really thought, for some seconds, I saw a dark figure near the chimney-piece, but I felt under my pillow for my charm, and the moment my fingers touched it, the figure disappeared, and I felt quite certain, only that I had it by me, that something frightful would have made its appearance, and, perhaps, throttled me, as it did those poor people we heard of.'

'Well, listen to me,' I began, and recounted my adventure, at the recital of which she appeared horrified.

'And had you the charm near you?' she asked, earnestly.

'No, I had dropped it into a china vase in the drawing-room, but I shall certainly take it with me to-night, as you have so much faith in it.'

At this distance of time I cannot tell you, or even understand, how I overcame my horror so effectually as to lie alone in my room that night. I remember distinctly that I pinned the charm to my pillow. I fell asleep almost immediately, and slept even more soundly than usual all night.

Next night I passed as well. My sleep was delightfully deep and dreamless. But I wakened with a sense of lassitude and melancholy, which, however, did not exceed a degree that was almost luxurious.

'Well, I told you so,' said Carmilla, when I described my quiet sleep, 'I had such delightful sleep myself last night; I pinned the charm to the breast of my night-dress. It was too far away the night before. I am quite sure it was all fancy, except the dreams. I used to think that evil spirits made dreams, but our doctor told me it is no such thing. Only a fever passing by, or some other malady, as they often do, he said, knocks at the door, and not being able to get in, passes on, with that alarm.'

'And what do you think the charm is?' said I.

'It has been fumigated or immersed in some drug, and is an antidote against the malaria,' she answered.

'Then it acts only on the body?'

'Certainly; you don't suppose that evil spirits are frightened by bits of ribbon, or the perfumes of a druggist's shop? No, these complaints, wandering in the air, begin by trying the nerves, and so infect the brain, but before they can seize upon you, the antidote repels them. That I am sure is what the charm has done for us. It is nothing magical, it is simply natural.'

I should have been happier if I could have quite agreed with Carmilla, but I did my best, and the impression was a little losing its force.

For some nights I slept profoundly; but still every morning I felt the same lassitude, and a languor weighed upon me all day.

I felt myself a changed girl. A strange melancholy was stealing over me, a melancholy that I would not have interrupted. Dim thoughts of death began to open, and an idea that I was slowly sinking took gentle, and, somehow, not unwelcome, possession of me. If it was sad, the tone of mind which this induced was also sweet. Whatever it might be, my soul acquiesced in it.

I would not admit that I was ill, I would not consent to tell my papa, or to have the doctor sent for.

Carmilla became more devoted to me than ever, and her strange paroxysms of languid adoration more frequent. She used to gloat on me with increasing ardour the more my strength and spirits waned. This always shocked me like a momentary glare of insanity.

Without knowing it, I was now in a pretty advanced stage of the strangest illness under which mortal ever suffered. There was an unaccountable fascination in its earlier symptoms that more than reconciled me to the incapacitating effect of that stage of the malady. This fascination increased for a time, until it reached a certain point, when gradually a sense of the horrible mingled itself with it, deepening, as you shall hear, until it discoloured and perverted the whole state of my life.

The first change I experienced was rather agreeable. It was very near the turning point from which began the descent of Avernus.[3]

Certain vague and strange sensations visited me in my sleep. The prevailing one was of that pleasant, peculiar cold thrill which we feel in bathing, when we move against the current of a river. This was soon accompanied by dreams that seemed interminable, and were so vague that I could never recollect their scenery and persons, or any one connected portion of their action. But they left an awful impression, and a sense of exhaustion, as if I had passed through a long period of great mental exertion and danger. After all these dreams there remained on waking a remembrance of having been in a place very nearly dark, and of having spoken to people whom I could not see; and especially of one clear voice, of a female's, very deep, that spoke as if at a distance, slowly, and producing always the same sensation of indescribable solemnity and fear. Sometimes there came a sensation as if a hand was drawn softly along my cheek and neck. Sometimes it was as if warm lips kissed me, and longer and more lovingly as they reached my throat, but there the caress fixed itself. My heart beat faster, my breathing rose and fell rapidly and full drawn; a sobbing, that rose into a sense of strangulation, supervened,[4] and turned into a dreadful convulsion, in which my senses left me and I became unconscious.

It was now three weeks since the commencement of this unaccountable state. My sufferings had, during the last week, told upon my appearance. I had grown pale, my eyes were dilated and darkened underneath, and the languor which I had long felt began to display itself in my countenance.[5]

My father asked me often whether I was ill; but, with an obstinacy which now seems to me unaccountable, I persisted in assuring him that I was quite well.

In a sense this was true. I had no pain, I could complain of no bodily derangement. My complaint seemed to be one of the imagination, or the nerves, and, horrible as my sufferings were, I kept them, with a morbid reserve, very nearly to myself.

It could not be that terrible complaint which the peasants called the oupire, for I had now been suffering for three weeks, and they were seldom ill for much more than three days, when death put an end to their miseries.

Carmilla complained of dreams and feverish sensations, but by no means of so alarming a kind as mine. I say that mine were extremely alarming. Had I been capable of comprehending my condition, I would have invoked aid and advice on my knees. The narcotic of an unsuspected influence was acting upon me, and my perceptions were benumbed.

I am going to tell you now of a dream that led immediately to an odd discovery.

One night, instead of the voice I was accustomed to hear in the dark, I heard one, sweet and tender, and at the same time terrible, which said, 'Your mother warns you to beware of the assassin.' At the same time a light unexpectedly sprang up, and I saw Carmilla, standing, near the foot of my bed, in her white night-dress, bathed, from her chin to her feet, in one great stain of blood.

I wakened with a shriek, possessed with the one idea that Carmilla was being murdered. I remember springing from my bed, and my next recollection is that of standing on the lobby, crying for help.

Madame and Mademoiselle came scurrying out of their rooms in alarm; a lamp burned always on the lobby, and seeing me, they soon learned the cause of my terror.

I insisted on our knocking at Carmilla's door. Our knocking was unanswered. It soon became a pounding and an uproar. We shrieked her name, but all was vain.

We all grew frightened, for the door was locked. We hurried back, in panic, to my room. There we rang the bell long and furiously. If my father's room had been at that side of the house, we would have called him up at once to our aid. But, alas! he was quite out of hearing, and to reach him involved an excursion for which we none of us had courage.

Servants, however, soon came running up the stairs; I had got on my dressing-gown and slippers meanwhile, and my companions were already similarly furnished. Recognising the voices of the servants on the lobby, we sallied out together; and having renewed, as fruitlessly, our summons at Carmilla's door, I ordered the men to force the lock. They did so, and we stood, holding our lights aloft, in the doorway, and so stared into the room.

We called her by name; but there was still no reply. We looked round the room. Everything was undisturbed. It was exactly in the state in which I had left it on bidding her good night. But Carmilla was gone.

CHAPTER VIII.

Search.

At sight of the room, perfectly undisturbed except for our violent entrance, we began to cool a little, and soon recovered our senses sufficiently to dismiss the men. It had struck Mademoiselle that possibly Carmilla had been wakened by the uproar at her door, and in her first panic had jumped from her bed, and hid herself in a press,[1] or behind a curtain, from which she could not, of course, emerge until the majordomo and his myrmidons[2] had withdrawn. We now recommenced our search, and began to call her name again.

It was all to no purpose. Our perplexity and agitation increased. We examined the windows, but they were secured. I implored of Carmilla, if she had concealed herself, to play this cruel trick no longer—to come out, and to end our anxieties. It was all useless. I was by this time convinced that she was not in the room, nor in the dressing room, the door of which was still locked on this side. She could not have passed it. I was utterly puzzled. Had Carmilla discovered one of those secret passages which the old house-keeper said were known to exist in the schloss, although the tradition of their exact situation had been lost. A little time would, no doubt, explain all—utterly perplexed as, for the present, we were.

It was past four o'clock, and I preferred passing the remaining hours of darkness in Madame's room. Daylight brought no solution of the difficulty.

The whole household, with my father at its head, was in a state of agitation next morning. Every part of the château was searched. The grounds were explored. Not a trace of the missing lady could be discovered. The stream was about to be dragged; my father was in distraction; what a tale to have to tell the poor girl's mother on her return. I, too, was almost beside myself, though my grief was quite of a different kind.

The morning was passed in alarm and excitement. It was now one o'clock, and still no tidings. I ran up to Carmilla's room, and found her standing at her dressing-table. I was astounded. I could not believe my eyes. She beckoned me to her with her pretty finger, in silence. Her face expressed extreme fear.

I ran to her in an ecstasy of joy; I kissed and embraced her again and again. I ran to the bell and rang it vehemently, to bring others to the spot, who might at once relieve my father's anxiety.

'Dear Carmilla, what has become of you all this time? We have been in agonies of anxiety about you,' I exclaimed. 'Where have you been? How did you come back?'

'Last night has been a night of wonders,' she said.

'For mercy's sake, explain all you can.'

'It was past two last night,' she said, 'when I went to sleep as usual in my bed, with my doors locked, that of the dressing-room, and that opening upon the gallery. My sleep was uninterrupted, and, so far as I know, dreamless; but I awoke just now on the sofa in the dressing-room there, and I found the door between the rooms open, and the other door forced. How could all this have happened without my being wakened? It must have been accompanied with a great deal of noise, and I am particularly easily wakened; and how could I have been carried out of my bed without my sleep having been interrupted, I whom the slightest stir startles?'

By this time, Madame, Mademoiselle, my father, and a number of the servants were in the room. Carmilla was, of course, overwhelmed with inquiries, congratulations, and welcomes. She had but one story to tell, and seemed the least able of all the party to suggest any way of accounting for what had happened.

My father took a turn up and down the room, thinking. I saw Carmilla's eye follow him for a moment with a sly, dark glance.

When my father had sent the servants away, Mademoiselle having gone in search of a little bottle of valerian and sal-volatile,[3] and there being no one now in the room with Carmilla, except my father, Madame, and myself, he came to her thoughtfully, took her hand very kindly, led her to the sofa, and sat down beside her.

'Will you forgive me, my dear, if I risk a conjecture, and ask a question?'

'Who can have a better right?' she said. 'Ask what you please, and I will tell you everything. But my story is simply one of bewilderment and darkness. I know absolutely nothing. Put any question you please. But you know, of course, the limitations mamma has placed me under.'

'Perfectly, my dear child. I need not approach the topics on which she desires our silence. Now, the marvel of last night consists in your having been removed from your bed and your room, without being wakened, and this removal having occurred apparently while the windows were still secured, and the two doors locked upon the inside. I will tell you my theory, and first ask you a question.'

Carmilla was leaning on her hand dejectedly; Madame and I were listening breathlessly.

'Now, my question is this. Have you ever been suspected of walking in your sleep?'

'Never, since I was very young indeed.'

'But you did walk in your sleep when you were young?'

'Yes; I know I did. I have been told so often by my old nurse.'

My father smiled and nodded.

'Well, what has happened is this. You got up in your sleep, unlocked the door, not leaving the key, as usual, in the lock, but taking it out and locking it on the outside; you again took the key out, and carried it away with you to some one of the five-and-twenty rooms on this floor, or perhaps up-stairs or down-stairs. There are so many rooms and closets, so much heavy furniture, and such accumulations of lumber, that it would re-quire a week to search this old house thoroughly. Do you see, now, what I mean?'

'I do, but not all,' she answered.

'And how, papa, do you account for her finding herself on the sofa in the dressing-room, which we had searched so carefully?'

'She came there after you had searched it, still in her sleep, and at last awoke spontaneously, and was as much surprised to find herself where she was as any one else. I wish all mysteries were as easily and innocently explained as yours, Carmilla,' he said, laughing. 'And so we may congratulate ourselves on the certainty that the most natural explanation of the occurrence is one that involves no drugging, no tampering with locks, no bur-glars, or poisoners, or witches—nothing that need alarm Car-milla, or any one else, for our safety.'

Carmilla was looking charmingly. Nothing could be more beautiful than her tints. Her beauty was, I think, enhanced by that graceful languor that was peculiar to her. I think my father was silently contrasting her looks with mine, for he said:

'I wish my poor Laura was looking more like herself;' and he sighed.

So our alarms were happily ended, and Carmilla restored to her friends.

CHAPTER IX.

The Doctor.

As Carmilla would not hear of an attendant sleeping in her room, my father arranged that a servant should sleep outside her door, so that she could not attempt to make another such excursion without being arrested at her own door.

That night passed quietly; and next morning early, the doctor, whom my father had sent for without telling me a word about it, arrived to see me.

Madame accompanied me to the library; and there the grave little doctor, with white hair and spectacles, whom I mentioned before, was waiting to receive me.

I told him my story, and as I proceeded he grew graver and graver.

We were standing, he and I, in the recess of one of the windows, facing one another. When my statement was over, he leaned with his shoulders against the wall, and with his eyes fixed on me earnestly, with an interest in which was a dash of horror.

After a minute's reflection, he asked Madame if he could see my father.

He was sent for accordingly, and as he entered, smiling, he said:

'I dare say, doctor, you are going to tell me that I am an old fool for having brought you here; I hope I am.'

But his smile faded into shadow as the doctor, with a very grave face, beckoned him to him.

He and the doctor talked for some time in the same recess where I had just conferred with the physician. It seemed an earnest and argumentative conversation. The room is very large, and I and Madame stood together, burning with curiosity, at the further end. Not a word could we hear, however, for they spoke in a very low tone, and the deep recess of the window quite concealed the doctor from view, and very nearly my father, whose foot, arm, and shoulder only could we see; and the voices were, I suppose, all the less audible for the sort of closet which the thick wall and window formed.

After a time my father's face looked into the room; it was pale, thoughtful, and, I fancied, agitated.

'Laura, dear, come here for a moment. Madame, we shan't trouble you, the doctor says, at present.'

Accordingly I approached, for the first time a little alarmed; for, although I felt very weak, I did not feel ill; and strength, one always fancies, is a thing that may be picked up when we please.

My father held out his hand to me, as I drew near, but he was looking at the doctor, and he said:

'It certainly *is* very odd; I don't understand it quite. Laura, come here, dear; now attend to Doctor Spielsberg, and recollect yourself.'

'You mentioned a sensation like that of two needles piercing the skin, somewhere about your neck, on the night when you experienced your first horrible dream. Is there still any soreness?'

'None at all,' I answered.

'Can you indicate with your finger about the point at which you think this occurred?'

'Very little below my throat—*here*,' I answered.

I wore a morning dress, which covered the place I pointed to.

'Now you can satisfy yourself,' said the doctor. 'You won't mind your papa's lowering your dress a very little. It is necessary, to detect a symptom of the complaint under which you have been suffering.'

I acquiesced. It was only an inch or two below the edge of my collar.

'God bless me!—so it is,' exclaimed my father, growing pale.

'You see it now with your own eyes,' said the doctor, with a gloomy triumph.

'What is it?' I exclaimed, beginning to be frightened.

'Nothing, my dear young lady, but a small blue spot, about the size of the tip of your little finger;[1] and now,' he continued, turning to papa, 'the question is what is best to be done?'

'Is there any danger?' I urged, in great trepidation.

'I trust not, my dear,' answered the doctor. 'I don't see why you should not recover. I don't see why you should not begin *immediately* to get better. That is the point at which the sense of strangulation begins?'

'Yes,' I answered.

'And—recollect as well as you can—the same point was a kind of centre of that thrill which you described just now, like the current of a cold stream running against you?'

'It may have been; I think it was.'

'Ay, you see?' he added, turning to my father. 'Shall I say a word to Madame?'

'Certainly,' said my father.

He called Madame to him, and said:

'I find my young friend here far from well. It won't be of any great consequence, I hope; but it will be necessary that some steps be taken, which I will explain by-and-bye; but in the meantime,

Madame, you will be so good as not to let Miss Laura be alone for one moment. That is the only direction I need give for the present. It is indispensable.'

'We may rely upon your kindness, Madame, I know,' added my father.

Madame satisfied him eagerly.

'And you, dear Laura, I know you will observe the doctor's direction.'

'I shall have to ask your opinion upon another patient, whose symptoms slightly resemble those of my daughter, that have just been detailed to you—very much milder in degree, but I believe quite of the same sort. She is a young lady—our guest; but as you say you will be passing this way again this evening, you can't do better than take your supper here, and you can then see her. She does not come down till the afternoon.'

'I thank you,' said the doctor. 'I shall be with you, then, at about seven this evening.'

And then they repeated their directions to me and to Madame, and with this parting charge my father left us, and walked out with the doctor; and I saw them pacing together up and down between the road and the moat, on the grassy platform in front of the castle, evidently absorbed in earnest conversation.

The doctor did not return. I saw him mount his horse there, take his leave, and ride away eastward through the forest.

Nearly at the same time I saw the man arrive from Dranfeld with the letters, and dismount and hand the bag to my father.

In the meantime, Madame and I were both busy, lost in conjecture as to the reasons of the singular and earnest direction which the doctor and my father had concurred in imposing. Madame, as she afterwards told me, was afraid the doctor apprehended a sudden seizure, and that, without prompt assistance, I might either lose my life in a fit, or at least be seriously hurt.

This interpretation did not strike me; and I fancied, perhaps luckily for my nerves, that the arrangement was prescribed simply to secure a companion, who would prevent my taking too much exercise, or eating unripe fruit, or doing any of the fifty foolish things to which young people are supposed to be prone.

About half-an-hour after my father came in—he had a letter in his hand—and said:

'This letter had been delayed; it is from General Spielsdorf. He might have been here yesterday, he may not come till to-morrow, or he may be here to-day.'

He put the open letter into my hand; but he did not look pleased, as he used when a guest, especially one so much loved as the General, was coming. On the contrary, he looked as if he wished him at the bottom of the Red Sea. There was plainly something on his mind which he did not choose to divulge.

'Papa, darling, will you tell me this?' said I, suddenly laying my hand on his arm, and looking, I am sure, imploringly in his face.

'Perhaps,' he answered, smoothing my hair caressingly over my eyes.

'Does the doctor think me very ill?'

'No, dear; he thinks, if right steps are taken, you will be quite well again, at least, on the high road to a complete recovery, in a day or two,' he answered, a little drily. 'I wish our good friend, the General, had chosen any other time; that is, I wish you had been perfectly well to receive him.'

'But do tell me, papa,' I insisted, '*what* does he think is the matter with me?'

'Nothing; you must not plague me with questions,' he answered, with more irritation than I ever remember him to have displayed before; and seeing that I looked wounded, I suppose, he kissed me, and added, 'You shall know all about it in a day or two; that is, all that *I* know. In the meantime you are not to trouble your head about it.'

He turned and left the room, but came back before I had done wondering and puzzling over the oddity of all this; it was merely to say that he was going to Karnstein, and had ordered the carriage to be ready at twelve, and that I and Madame should accompany him; he was going to see the priest who lived near those picturesque grounds, upon business, and as Carmilla had never seen them, she could follow, when she came down, with Mademoiselle, who would bring materials for what you call a pic-nic, which might be laid for us in the ruined castle.

At twelve o'clock, accordingly, I was ready, and not long after, my father, Madame, and I set out upon our projected drive.

Passing the drawbridge we turn to the right, and follow the road over the steep gothic bridge, westward, to reach the deserted village and ruined castle of Karnstein.

No sylvan drive can be fancied prettier. The ground breaks into gentle hills and hollows, all clothed with beautiful wood, totally destitute of the comparative formality which artificial planting and early culture and pruning impart.

The irregularities of the ground often lead the road out of its course, and cause it to wind beautifully round the sides of broken hollows and the steeper sides of the hills, among varieties of ground almost inexhaustible.

Turning one of these points, we suddenly encountered our old friend, the General, riding towards us, attended by a mounted servant. His portmanteaus[2] were following in a hired waggon, such as we term a cart.

The General dismounted as we pulled up, and, after the usual greetings, was easily persuaded to accept the vacant seat in the carriage, and send his horse on with his servant to the schloss.

CHAPTER X.

Bereaved.

It was about ten months since we had last seen him; but that time had sufficed to make an alteration of years in his appearance. He had grown thinner; something of gloom and anxiety had taken the place of that cordial serenity which used to characterise his features. His dark blue eyes, always penetrating, now gleamed with a sterner light from under his shaggy grey eyebrows. It was not such a change as grief alone usually induces, and angrier passions seemed to have had their share in bringing it about.

We had not long resumed our drive, when the General began to talk, with his usual soldierly directness, of the bereavement, as he termed it, which he had sustained in the death of his beloved niece and ward; and he then broke out in a tone of intense bitterness and fury, inveighing against the 'hellish arts' to which she had fallen a victim, and expressing, with more exasperation than piety, his wonder that Heaven should tolerate so monstrous an indulgence of the lusts and malignity of hell.

My father, who saw at once that something very extraordinary had befallen, asked him, if not too painful to him, to detail the circumstances which he thought justified the strong terms in which he expressed himself.

'I should tell you all with pleasure,' said the General, 'but you would not believe me.'

'Why should I not?' he asked.

'Because,' he answered testily, 'you believe in nothing but what consists with your own prejudices and illusions. I remember when I was like you, but I have learned better.'

'Try me,' said my father; 'I am not such a dogmatist as you suppose. Besides which, I very well know that you generally require proof for what you believe, and am, therefore, very strongly pre-disposed to respect your conclusions.'

'You are right in supposing that I have not been led lightly into a belief in the marvellous—for what I have experienced *is* marvellous—and I have been forced by extraordinary evidence to credit that which ran counter, diametrically, to all my theories. I have been made the dupe of a preternatural conspiracy.'

Notwithstanding his professions of confidence in the General's penetration, I saw my father, at this point, glance at the General, with, as I thought, a marked suspicion of his sanity.

The General did not see it, luckily. He was looking gloomily and curiously into the glades and vistas of the woods that were opening before us.

'You are going to the Ruins of Karnstein?' he said. 'Yes, it is a lucky coincidence; do you know I was going to ask you to bring me there to inspect them. I have a special object in exploring. There is a ruined chapel, ain't there, with a great many tombs of that extinct family?'

'So there are—highly interesting,' said my father. 'I hope you are thinking of claiming the title and estates?'

My father said this gaily, but the General did not recollect the laugh, or even the smile, which courtesy exacts for a friend's joke; on the contrary, he looked grave and even fierce, ruminating on a matter that stirred his anger and horror.

'Something very different,' he said, gruffly. 'I mean to un-earth some of those fine people. I hope, by God's blessing, to ac-complish a pious sacrilege here, which will relieve our earth of certain monsters, and enable honest people to sleep in their beds without being assailed by murderers. I have strange things to tell you, my dear friend, such as I myself would have scouted as in-credible a few months since.'

My father looked at him again, but this time not with a glance of suspicion—with an eye, rather, of keen intelligence and alarm.

'The house of Karnstein,' he said, 'has been long extinct: a hundred years at least. My dear wife was maternally descended from the Karnsteins. But the name and title have long ceased to exist. The castle is a ruin; the very village is deserted; it is fifty years since the smoke of a chimney was seen there; not a roof left.'

'Quite true. I have heard a great deal about that since I last saw you; a great deal that will astonish you. But I had better re-late everything in the order in which it occurred,' said the Gen-eral. 'You saw my dear ward—my child, I may call her. No creature could have been more beautiful, and only three months ago none more blooming.'

'Yes, poor thing! when I saw her last she certainly was quite lovely,' said my father. 'I was grieved and shocked more than I can tell you, my dear friend; I knew what a blow it was to you.'

He took the General's hand, and they exchanged a kind pres-sure. Tears gathered in the old soldier's eyes. He did not seek to conceal them. He said:

'We have been very old friends; I knew you would feel for me, childless as I am. She had become an object of very near interest to me, and repaid my care by an affection that cheered my home and made my life happy. That is all gone. The years that remain to me on earth may not be very long; but by God's mercy I hope to accomplish a service to mankind before I die, and to sub-serve[1] the vengeance of Heaven upon the fiends who have mur-dered my poor child in the spring of her hopes and beauty!'

'You said, just now, that you intended relating everything as it occurred,' said my father. 'Pray do; I assure you that it is not mere curiosity that prompts me.'

By this time we had reached the point at which the Drunstall road, by which the General had come, diverges from the road which we were travelling to Karnstein.

'How far is it to the ruins?' enquired the General, looking anxiously forward.

'About half a league,' answered my father. 'Pray let us hear the story you were so good as to promise.'

The Story.

'With all my heart,' said the General, with an effort; and after a short pause in which to arrange his subject, he commenced one of the strangest narratives I had ever heard.

'My dear child was looking forward with great pleasure to the visit you had been so good as to arrange for her to your charming daughter.' Here he made me a gallant but melancholy bow. 'In the meantime we had an invitation to my old friend the Count Carlsfeld, whose schloss is about six leagues to the other side of Karnstein. It was to attend the series of fêtes which, you remember, were given by him in honour of his illustrious visitor, the Grand Duke Charles.'

'Yes; and very splendid, I believe, they were,' said my father.

'Princely! But then his hospitalities are quite regal. He has Aladdin's lamp.[1] The night from which my sorrow dates was devoted to a magnificent masquerade. The grounds were thrown open, the trees hung with coloured lamps. There was such a display of fireworks as Paris itself has never witnessed. And such music—music, you know, is my weakness—such ravishing music! The finest instrumental band, perhaps, in the world, and the finest singers who could be collected from all the great operas in Europe. As you wandered through these fantastically illuminated grounds, the moon-lighted château throwing a rosy light from its long rows of windows, you would suddenly hear these ravishing voices stealing from the silence of some grove, or rising from boats upon the lake. I felt myself, as I looked and listened, carried back into the romance and poetry of my early youth.

'When the fireworks were ended, and the ball beginning, we returned to the noble suite of rooms that were thrown open to the dancers. A masked ball, you know, is a beautiful sight; but so brilliant a spectacle of the kind I never saw before.

'It was a very aristocratic assembly. I was myself almost the only "nobody" present.

'My dear child was looking quite beautiful. She wore no mask. Her excitement and delight added an unspeakable charm to her features, always lovely. I remarked a young lady, dressed magnificently, but wearing a mask, who appeared to me to be observing my ward with extraordinary interest. I had seen her, earlier in the evening, in the great hall, and again, for a few minutes, walking near us, on the terrace under the castle windows, similarly employed. A lady, also masked, richly and gravely dressed, and with a stately air, like a person of rank, accompanied her as a chaperon. Had the young lady not worn a mask, I could, of course, have been much more certain upon the question whether she was really watching my poor darling. I am now well assured that she was.

'We were now in one of the *salons*. My poor dear child had been dancing, and was resting a little in one of the chairs near the door; I was standing near. The two ladies I have mentioned had approached, and the younger took the chair next my ward; while her companion stood beside me, and for a little time addressed herself, in a low tone, to her charge.

'Availing herself of the privilege of her mask, she turned to me, and in the tone of an old friend, and calling me by my name, opened a conversation with me, which piqued my curiosity a good deal. She referred to many scenes where she had met me— at Court, and at distinguished houses. She alluded to little incidents which I had long ceased to think of, but which, I found, had only lain in abeyance in my memory, for they instantly started into life at her touch.

'I became more and more curious to ascertain who she was, every moment. She parried my attempts to discover very adroitly and pleasantly. The knowledge she showed of many passages in my life seemed to me all but unaccountable; and she appeared to take a not unnatural pleasure in foiling my curiosity, and in seeing me flounder, in my eager perplexity, from one conjecture to another.

'In the meantime the young lady, whom her mother called by the odd name of Millarca, when she once or twice addressed her, had, with the same ease and grace, got into conversation with my ward.

'She introduced herself by saying that her mother was a very old acquaintance of mine. She spoke of the agreeable audacity which a mask rendered practicable; she talked like a friend; she admired her dress, and insinuated very prettily her admiration of her beauty. She amused her with laughing criticisms upon the people who crowded the ball-room, and laughed at my poor child's fun. She was very witty and lively when she pleased, and after a time they had grown very good friends, and the young stranger lowered her mask, displaying a remarkably beautiful face. I had never seen it before, neither had my dear child. But though it was new to us, the features were so engaging, as well as lovely, that it was impossible not to feel the attraction powerfully. My poor girl did so. I never saw anyone more taken with another at first sight, unless, indeed, it was the stranger herself, who seemed quite to have lost her heart to her.

'In the meantime, availing myself of the license of a masquerade, I put not a few questions to the elder lady.

'"You have puzzled me utterly," I said, laughing. "Is that not
enough? won't you, now, consent to stand on equal terms, and
do me the kindness to remove your mask?"

'"Can any request be more unreasonable?" she replied. "Ask
a lady to yield an advantage! Beside, how do you know you
should recognise me? Years make changes."

'"As you see," I said, with a bow, and, I suppose, a rather
melancholy little laugh.

'"As philosophers tell us," she said; "and how do you know
that a sight of my face would help you?"

'"I should take chance for that," I answered. "It is vain trying
to make yourself out an old woman; your figure betrays you."

'"Years, nevertheless, have passed since I saw you, rather
since you saw me, for that is what I am considering. Millarca,
there, is my daughter; I cannot then be young, even in the opinion of people whom time has taught to be indulgent, and I may
not like to be compared with what you remember me.² You have
no mask to remove. You can offer me nothing in exchange."

'"My petition is to your pity, to remove it."

'"And mine to yours, to let it stay where it is," she replied.

'"Well, then, at least you will tell me whether you are French
or German; you speak both languages so perfectly."

'"I don't think I shall tell you that, General; you intend a surprise, and are meditating the particular point of attack."

'"At all events, you won't deny this," I said, "that being hon-
oured by your permission to converse, I ought to know how to
address you. Shall I say Madame la Comtesse?"

'She laughed, and she would, no doubt, have met me with another evasion—if, indeed, I can treat any occurrence in an interview every circumstance of which was pre-arranged, as I now

believe, with the profoundest cunning, as liable to be modified by accident.

'"As to that," she began; but she was interrupted, almost as she opened her lips, by a gentleman, dressed in black, who looked particularly elegant and distinguished, with this drawback, that his face was the most deadly pale I ever saw, except in death. He was in no masquerade—in the plain evening dress of a gentleman; and he said, without a smile, but with a courtly and unusually low bow:—

'"Will Madame la Comtesse permit me to say a very few words which may interest her?"

'The lady turned quickly to him, and touched her lip in token of silence; she then said to me, "Keep my place for me, General; I shall return when I have said a few words."

'And with this injunction, playfully given, she walked a little aside with the gentleman in black, and talked for some minutes, apparently very earnestly. They then walked away slowly together in the crowd, and I lost them for some minutes.

'I spent the interval in cudgelling my brains for a conjecture as to the identity of the lady who seemed to remember me so kindly, and I was thinking of turning about and joining in the conversation between my pretty ward and the Countess's daughter, and trying whether, by the time she returned, I might not have a surprise in store for her, by having her name, title, château, and estates at my fingers' ends. But at this moment she returned, accompanied by the pale man in black, who said:

'"I shall return and inform Madame la Comtesse when her carriage is at the door."

'He withdrew with a bow.'

CHAPTER XII.

A Petition.

'"Then we are to lose Madame la Comtesse, but I hope only for a few hours," I said, with a low bow.

'"It may be that only, or it may be a few weeks. It was very unlucky his speaking to me just now as he did. Do you now know me?"

'I assured her I did not.

'"You shall know me," she said, "but not at present. We are older and better friends than, perhaps, you suspect. I cannot yet declare myself. I shall in three weeks pass your beautiful schloss, about which I have been making enquiries. I shall then look in upon you for an hour or two, and renew a friendship which I never think of without a thousand pleasant recollections. This moment a piece of news has reached me like a thunderbolt. I must set out now, and travel by a devious[1] route, nearly a hundred miles, with all the dispatch I can possibly make. My perplexities multiply. I am only deterred by the compulsory reserve I practise as to my name from making a very singular request of you. My poor child has not quite recovered her strength. Her horse fell with her, at a hunt which she had ridden out to witness, her nerves have not yet recovered the shock, and our physician says that she must on no account exert herself for some time to come. We came here, in consequence, by very easy stages—hardly six leagues a day. I must now travel day and night, on a mission of life and death—a mission the critical and momentous nature of which I shall be able to explain to you when we meet, as I hope we shall, in a few weeks, without the necessity of any concealment."

'She went on to make her petition, and it was in the tone of a person from whom such a request amounted to conferring, rather than seeking a favour. This was only in manner, and, as it seemed, quite unconsciously. Than the terms in which it was expressed, nothing could be more deprecatory. It was simply that I would consent to take charge of her daughter during her absence.

'This was, all things considered, a strange, not to say, an audacious request. She in some sort disarmed me, by stating and admitting everything that could be urged against it, and throwing herself entirely upon my chivalry. At the same moment, by a fatality that seems to have predetermined all that happened, my poor child came to my side, and, in an undertone, besought me to invite her new friend, Millarca, to pay us a visit. She had just been sounding her, and thought, if her mamma would allow her, she would like it extremely.

'At another time I should have told her to wait a little, until, at least, we knew who they were. But I had not a moment to think in. The two ladies assailed me together, and I must confess the refined and beautiful face of the young lady, about which there was something extremely engaging, as well as the elegance and fire of high birth, determined me; and, quite overpowered, I submitted, and undertook, too easily, the care of the young lady, whom her mother called Millarca.

'The Countess beckoned to her daughter, who listened with grave attention while she told her, in general terms, how sud-

denly and peremptorily she had been summoned, and also of the
arrangement she had made for her under my care, adding that I
was one of her earliest and most valued friends.

'I made, of course, such speeches as the case seemed to call
for, and found myself, on reflection, in a position which I did
not half like.

'The gentleman in black returned, and very ceremoniously
conducted the lady from the room.

'The demeanor of this gentleman was such as to impress me
with the conviction that the Countess was a lady of very much
more importance than her modest title alone might have led me
to assume.

'Her last charge to me was that no attempt was to be made to
learn more about her than I might have already guessed, until
her return. Our distinguished host, whose guest she was, knew
her reasons.

'"But here," she said, "neither I nor my daughter could safely
remain for more than a day. I removed my mask imprudently for
a moment, about an hour ago, and, too late, I fancied you saw
me. So I resolved to seek an opportunity of talking a little to
you. Had I found that you *had* seen me, I should have thrown
myself on your high sense of honour to keep my secret for some
weeks. As it is, I am satisfied that you did not see me; but if
you now *suspect*, or, on reflection, *should* suspect, who I am,
I commit myself, in like manner, entirely to your honour. My
daughter will observe the same secresy, and I well know that
you will, from time to time, remind her, lest she should thought-
lessly disclose it."

'She whispered a few words to her daughter, kissed her hur-
riedly twice, and went away, accompanied by the pale gentleman
in black, and disappeared in the crowd.

'"In the next room," said Millarca, "there is a window that

looks upon the hall door. I should like to see the last of mamma, and to kiss my hand to her."

'We assented, of course, and accompanied her to the window. We looked out, and saw a handsome old-fashioned carriage, with a troop of couriers and footmen. We saw the slim figure of the pale gentleman in black, as he held a thick velvet cloak, and placed it about her shoulders and threw the hood over her head. She nodded to him, and just touched his hand with hers. He bowed low repeatedly as the door closed, and the carriage began to move.

'"She is gone," said Millarca, with a sigh.

'"She is gone," I repeated to myself, for the first time—in the hurried moments that had elapsed since my consent—reflecting upon the folly of my act.

'"She did not look up," said the young lady, plaintively.

'"The Countess had taken off her mask, perhaps, and did not care to show her face," I said; "and she could not know that you were in the window."

'She sighed, and looked in my face. She was so beautiful that I relented. I was sorry I had for a moment repented of my hospitality, and I determined to make her amends for the unavowed churlishness of my reception.

'The young lady, replacing her mask, joined my ward in persuading me to return to the grounds, where the concert was soon to be renewed. We did so, and walked up and down the terrace that lies under the castle windows. Millarca became very intimate with us, and amused us with lively descriptions and stories of most of the great people whom we saw upon the terrace. I liked her more and more every minute. Her gossip, without being ill-natured, was extremely diverting to me, who had been so long out of the great world. I thought what life she would give to our sometimes lonely evenings at home.

'This ball was not over until the morning sun had almost reached the horizon. It pleased the Grand Duke to dance till then, so loyal people could not go away, or think of bed.

'We had just got through a crowded saloon, when my ward asked me what had become of Millarca. I thought she had been by her side, and she fancied she was by mine. The fact was, we had lost her.

'All my efforts to find her were vain. I feared that she had mistaken, in the confusion of a momentary separation from us, other people for her new friends, and had, possibly, pursued and lost them in the extensive grounds which were thrown open to us.

'Now, in its full force, I recognised a new folly in my having undertaken the charge of a young lady without so much as knowing her name; and fettered as I was by promises, of the reasons for imposing which I knew nothing, I could not even point my inquiries by saying that the missing young lady was the daughter of the Countess who had taken her departure a few hours before.

'Morning broke. It was clear daylight before I gave up my search. It was not till near two o'clock next day that we heard anything of my missing charge.

'At about that time a servant knocked at my niece's door, to say that he had been earnestly requested by a young lady, who appeared to be in great distress, to make out where she could find the General Baron Spielsdorf and the young lady his daughter, in whose charge she had been left by her mother.

'There could be no doubt, notwithstanding the slight inaccuracy, that our young friend had turned up; and so she had. Would to heaven we had lost her!

'She told my poor child a story to account for her having failed to recover us for so long. Very late, she said, she had got

to the housekeeper's bedroom in despair of finding us, and had
then fallen into a deep sleep which, long as it was, had hardly
sufficed to recruit her strength after the fatigues of the ball.

'That day Millarca came home with us. I was only too
happy, after all, to have secured so charming a companion for
my dear girl.

CHAPTER XIII

The Wood-Man.

'There soon, however, appeared some drawbacks. In the first place, Millarca complained of extreme languor—the weakness that remained after her late illness—and she never emerged from her room till the afternoon was pretty far advanced. In the next place, it was accidentally discovered, although she always locked her door on the inside, and never disturbed the key from its place till she admitted the maid to assist at her toilet, that she was undoubtedly sometimes absent from her room in the very early morning, and at various times later in the day, before she wished it to be understood that she was stirring. She was repeatedly seen from the windows of the schloss, in the first faint grey of the morning, walking through the trees, in an easterly direction, and looking like a person in a trance. This convinced me that she walked in her sleep. But this hypothesis did not solve the puzzle. How did she pass out from her room, leaving the door locked on the inside? How did she escape from the house without unbarring door or window?

'In the midst of my perplexities, an anxiety of a far more urgent kind presented itself.

'My dear child began to lose her looks and health, and that in a manner so mysterious, and even horrible, that I became thoroughly frightened.

'She was at first visited by appalling dreams; then, as she fancied, by a spectre, sometimes resembling Millarca, sometimes in the shape of a beast, indistinctly seen, walking round the foot of her bed, from side to side. Lastly came sensations. One, not unpleasant, but very peculiar, she said, resembled the flow of an icy stream against her breast. At a later time, she felt something like a pair of large needles pierce her, a little below the throat, with a very sharp pain. A few nights after, followed a gradual and convulsive sense of strangulation; then came unconsciousness.'[1]

I could hear distinctly every word the kind old General was saying, because by this time we were driving upon the short grass that spreads on either side of the road as you approach the roofless village which had not shown the smoke of a chimney for more than half a century.

You may guess how strangely I felt as I heard my own symptoms so exactly described in those which had been experienced by the poor girl who, but for the catastrophe which followed, would have been at that moment a visitor at my father's château. You may suppose, also, how I felt as I heard him detail habits and mysterious peculiarities which were, in fact, those of our beautiful guest, Carmilla!

A vista opened in the forest; we were on a sudden under the chimneys and gables of the ruined village, and the towers and battlements of the dismantled castle, round which gigantic trees are grouped, overhung us from a slight eminence.

In a frightened dream I got down from the carriage, and in silence, for we had each abundant matter for thinking; we soon mounted the ascent, and were among the spacious chambers, winding stairs, and dark corridors of the castle.

'And this was once the palatial residence of the Karnsteins!' said the old General at length, as from a great window he looked out across the village, and saw the wide, undulating expanse of forest. 'It was a bad family, and here its bloodstained annals were written,' he continued. 'It is hard that they should, after death, continue to plague the human race with their atrocious lusts. That is the chapel of the Karnsteins, down there.'

He pointed down to the grey walls of the gothic building, partly visible through the foliage, a little way down the steep. 'And I hear the axe of a woodman,' he added, 'busy among the trees that surround it; he possibly may give us the information of which I am in search, and point out the grave of Mircalla, Countess of Karnstein. These rustics preserve the local traditions of great families, whose stories die out among the rich and titled so soon as the families themselves become extinct.'

'We have a portrait, at home, of Mircalla, the Countess Karnstein; should you like to see it?' asked my father.

'Time enough, dear friend,' replied the General. 'I believe that I have seen the original; and one motive which has led me to you earlier than I at first intended, was to explore the chapel which we are now approaching.'

'What! see the Countess Mircalla,' exclaimed my father; 'why, she has been dead more than a century!'

'Not so dead as you fancy, I am told,' answered the General.

'I confess, General, you puzzle me utterly,' replied my father, looking at him, I fancied, for a moment with a return of the suspicion I detected before. But although there was anger and detestation, at times, in the old General's manner, there was nothing flighty.

'There remains to me,' he said, as we passed under the heavy arch of the gothic church—for its dimensions would have justified its being so styled—'but one object which can interest me during the few years that remain to me on earth, and that is to wreak on her the vengeance which, I thank God, may still be accomplished by a mortal arm.'

'What vengeance can you mean?' asked my father, in increasing amazement.

'I mean, to decapitate the monster,' he answered, with a fierce flush, and a stamp that echoed mournfully through the hollow ruin, and his clenched hand was at the same moment raised, as if it grasped the handle of an axe, while he shook it ferociously in the air.

'What?' exclaimed my father, more than ever bewildered.

'To strike her head off.'

'Cut her head off!'

'Aye, with a hatchet, with a spade, or with anything that can cleave through her murderous throat. You shall hear,' he answered, trembling with rage. And hurrying forward he said:

'That beam will answer for a seat; your dear child is fatigued; let her be seated, and I will, in a few sentences, close my dreadful story.'

The squared block of wood, which lay on the grass-grown pavement of the chapel, formed a bench on which I was very glad to seat myself, and in the meantime the General called to the woodman, who had been removing some boughs which leaned upon the old walls; and, axe in hand, the hardy old fellow stood before us.

He could not tell us anything of these monuments; but there was an old man, he said, a ranger of this forest, at present sojourning in the house of the priest, about two miles away, who could point out every monument of the old Karnstein family; and, for a trifle, he undertook to bring him back with him, if we would lend him one of our horses, in little more than half-an-hour.

'Have you been long employed about this forest?' asked my father of the old man.

'I have been a woodman here,' he answered in his *patois*, 'under the forester, all my days; so has my father before me, and so on, as many generations as I can count up. I could show you the very house, in the village here, in which my ancestors lived.'

'How came the village to be deserted?' asked the General.

'It was troubled by *revenants*,[2] sir; several were tracked to their graves, there detected by the usual tests,[3] and extinguished in the usual way, by decapitation, by the stake, and by burning; but not until many of the villagers were killed.

'But after all these proceedings according to law,' he continued—'so many graves opened, and so many vampires deprived of their horrible animation—the village was not relieved. But a Moravian[4] nobleman, who happened to be travelling this way, heard how matters were, and being skilled—as many people are in his country—in such affairs, he offered to deliver the village from its tormentor. He did so thus: There being a bright moon that night, he ascended, shortly after sunset, the towers of the chapel here, from whence he could distinctly see the churchyard beneath him; you can see it from that window. From this point he watched until he saw the vampire come out of his grave, and place near it the linen clothes in which he had been folded, and then glide away towards the village to plague its inhabitants.

'The stranger, having seen all this, came down from the steeple, took the linen wrappings of the vampire, and carried them up to the top of the tower, which he again mounted. When the vampire returned from his prowlings and missed his clothes, he cried furiously to the Moravian, whom he saw at the summit of the tower, and who, in reply, beckoned him to ascend and take them. Whereupon the vampire, accepting his invitation, began

to climb the steeple, and so soon as he had reached the battlements, the Moravian, with a stroke of his sword, clove his skull
in twain, hurling him down to the churchyard, whither, descending by the winding stairs, the stranger followed and cut his
head off, and next day delivered it and the body to the villagers,
who duly impaled and burnt them.

'This Moravian nobleman had authority from the then head
of the family to remove the tomb of Mircalla, Countess Karnstein, which he did effectually, so that in a little while its site was
quite forgotten.'

'Can you point out where it stood?' asked the General, eagerly.

The forester shook his head, and smiled.

'Not a soul living could tell you that now,' he said; 'besides,
they say her body was removed; but no one is sure of that either.'

Having thus spoken, as time pressed, he dropped his axe and
departed, leaving us to hear the remainder of the General's
strange story.

CHAPTER XIV.

The Meeting.

'My beloved child,' he resumed, 'was now growing rapidly worse. The physician who attended her had failed to produce the slightest impression upon her disease, for such I then supposed it to be. He saw my alarm, and suggested a consultation. I called in an abler physician, from Gratz. Several days elapsed before he arrived. He was a good and pious, as well as a learned man. Having seen my poor ward together, they withdrew to my library to confer and discuss. I, from the adjoining room, where I awaited their summons, heard these two gentlemen's voices raised in something sharper than a strictly philosophical discussion. I knocked at the door and entered. I found the old physician from Gratz maintaining his theory. His rival was combating it with undisguised ridicule, accompanied with bursts of laughter. This unseemly manifestation subsided and the altercation ended on my entrance.

'"Sir," said my first physician, "my learned brother seems to think that you want a conjuror, and not a doctor."

'"Pardon me," said the old physician from Gratz, looking displeased, "I shall state my own view of the case in my own way another time. I grieve, Monsieur le Général, that by my skill and science I can be of no use. Before I go I shall do myself the honour to suggest something to you."

'He seemed thoughtful, and sat down at a table and began to
write. Profoundly disappointed, I made my bow, and as I turned
to go, the other doctor pointed over his shoulder to his companion who was writing, and then, with a shrug, significantly
touched his forehead.

'This consultation, then, left me precisely where I was. I
walked out into the grounds, all but distracted. The doctor from
Gratz, in ten or fifteen minutes, overtook me. He apologized for
having followed me, but said that he could not conscientiously
take his leave without a few words more. He told me that he
could not be mistaken; no natural disease exhibited the same
symptoms; and that death was already very near. There remained, however, a day, or possibly two, of life. If the fatal seizure were at once arrested, with great care and skill her strength
might possibly return. But all hung now upon the confines of the
irrevocable. One more assault might extinguish the last spark of
vitality which is, every moment, ready to die.

'"And what is the nature of the seizure you speak of?" I entreated.

'"I have stated all fully in this note, which I place in your
hands upon the distinct condition that you send for the nearest
clergyman, and open my letter in his presence, and on no account read it till he is with you; you would despise it else, and it
is a matter of life and death. Should the priest fail you, then, indeed, you may read it."

'He asked me, before taking his leave finally, whether I would
wish to see a man curiously learned upon the very subject,
which, after I had read his letter, would probably interest me
above all others, and he urged me earnestly to invite him to visit
him there; and so took his leave.

'The ecclesiastic was absent, and I read the letter by myself.
At another time, or in another case, it might have excited my

ridicule. But into what quackeries will not people rush for a last chance, where all accustomed means have failed, and the life of a beloved object is at stake?

'Nothing, you will say, could be more absurd than the learned man's letter. It was monstrous enough to have consigned him to a madhouse. He said that the patient was suffering from the visits of a vampire! The punctures which she described as having occurred near the throat, were, he insisted, the insertion of those two long, thin, and sharp teeth which, it is well known, are peculiar to vampires; and there could be no doubt, he added, as to the well-defined presence of the small livid mark which all concurred in describing as that induced by the demon's lips, and every symptom described by the sufferer was in exact conformity with those recorded in every case of a similar visitation.

'Being myself wholly sceptical as to the existence of any such portent as the vampire, the supernatural theory of the good doctor furnished, in my opinion, but another instance of learning and intelligence oddly associated with some one hallucination. I was so miserable, however, that, rather than try nothing, I acted upon the instructions of the letter.

'I concealed myself in the dark dressing-room, that opened upon the poor patient's room, in which a candle was burning, and watched there till she was fast asleep. I stood at the door, peeping through the small crevice, my sword laid on the table beside me, as my directions prescribed, until, a little after one, I saw a large black object, very ill-defined, crawl, as it seemed to me, over the foot of the bed, and swiftly spread itself up to the poor girl's throat, where it swelled, in a moment, into a great, palpitating mass.

'For a few moments I had stood petrified. I now sprang forward, with my sword in my hand. The black creature suddenly contracted toward the foot of the bed, glided over it, and, standing on the floor about a yard below the foot of the bed, with a glare of skulking ferocity and horror fixed on me, I saw Millarca. Speculating I know not what, I struck at her instantly with my sword; but I saw her standing near the door, unscathed. Horrified, I pursued, and struck again. She was gone; and my sword flew to shivers against the door.

'I can't describe to you all that passed on that horrible night. The whole house was up and stirring. The spectre Millarca was gone. But her victim was sinking fast, and before the morning dawned, she died.'

The old General was agitated. We did not speak to him. My father walked to some little distance, and began reading the inscriptions on the tombstones; and thus occupied, he strolled into the door of a side-chapel to prosecute his researches. The General leaned against the wall, dried his eyes, and sighed heavily. I was relieved on hearing the voices of Carmilla and Madame, who were at that moment approaching. The voices died away.

In this solitude, having just listened to so strange a story, connected, as it was, with the great and titled dead, whose monuments were mouldering among the dust and ivy round us, and every incident of which bore so awfully upon my own mysterious case—in this haunted spot, darkened by the towering foliage that rose on every side, dense and high above its noiseless walls—a horror began to steal over me, and my heart sank as I thought that my friends were, after all, not about to enter and disturb this triste[1] and ominous scene.

The old General's eyes were fixed on the ground, as he leaned with his hand upon the basement[2] of a shattered monument.

Under a narrow, arched doorway, surmounted by one of those demoniacal grotesques in which the cynical and ghastly fancy of old Gothic carving delights, I saw very gladly the beautiful face and figure of Carmilla enter the shadowy chapel.

I was just about to rise and speak, and nodded smiling, in answer to her peculiarly engaging smile; when with a cry, the old man by my side caught up the woodman's hatchet, and started forward. On seeing him a brutalised change came over her features. It was an instantaneous and horrible transformation, as she made a crouching step backwards. Before I could utter a scream, he struck at her with all his force, but she dived under his blow, and unscathed, caught him in her tiny grasp by the wrist. He struggled for a moment to release his arm, but his hand opened, the axe fell to the ground, and the girl was gone.

He staggered against the wall. His grey hair stood upon his head, and a moisture shone over his face, as if he were at the point of death.

The frightful scene had passed in a moment. The first thing I recollect after, is Madame standing before me, and impatiently repeating again and again, the question, 'Where is Mademoiselle Carmilla?'

I answered at length, 'I don't know—I can't tell—she went there,' and I pointed to the door through which Madame had just entered; 'only a minute or two since.'

'But I have been standing there, in the passage, ever since Mademoiselle Carmilla entered; and she did not return.'

She then began to call 'Carmilla,' through every door and passage and from the windows, but no answer came.

'She called herself Carmilla?' asked the General, still agitated.

'Carmilla, yes,' I answered.

'Aye,' he said; 'that is Millarca. That is the same person who long ago was called Mircalla, Countess Karnstein. Depart from this accursed ground, my poor child, as quickly as you can. Drive to the clergyman's house, and stay there till we come. Begone! May you never behold Carmilla more; you will not find her here.'

Ordeal and Execution.

As he spoke one of the strangest looking men I ever beheld, entered the chapel at the door through which Carmilla had made her entrance and her exit. He was tall, narrow-chested, stooping, with high shoulders, and dressed in black. His face was brown and dried in with deep furrows; he wore an oddly-shaped hat with a broad leaf.[1] His hair, long and grizzled, hung on his shoulders. He wore a pair of gold spectacles, and walked slowly, with an odd shambling gait, with his face sometimes turned up to the sky, and sometimes bowed down toward the ground, seemed to wear a perpetual smile; his long thin arms were swinging, and his lank hands, in old black gloves ever so much too wide for them, waving and gesticulating in utter abstraction.

'The very man!' exclaimed the General, advancing with manifest delight. 'My dear Baron, how happy I am to see you, I had no hope of meeting you so soon.' He signed to my father, who had by this time returned, and leading the fantastic old gentleman, whom he called the Baron to meet him. He introduced him formally, and they at once entered into earnest conversation. The stranger took a roll of paper from his pocket, and spread it on the worn surface of a tomb that stood by. He had a pencil case in his fingers, with which he traced imaginary lines from point to point on the paper, which from their often glancing from it, together, at certain points of the building, I concluded to be a plan of the chapel. He accompanied, what I may term, his lecture, with occasional readings from a dirty little book, whose yellow leaves were closely written over.

They sauntered together down the side aisle, opposite to the spot where I was standing, conversing as they went; then they begun measuring distances by paces, and finally they all stood together, facing a piece of the side-wall, which they began to examine with great minuteness; pulling off the ivy that clung over it, and rapping the plaster with the ends of their sticks, scraping here, and knocking there. At length they ascertained the existence of a broad marble tablet, with letters carved in relief upon it.

With the assistance of the woodman, who soon returned, a monumental inscription, and carved escutcheon,[2] were disclosed. They proved to be those of the long lost monument of Mircalla, Countess Karnstein.

The old General, though not I fear given to the praying mood, raised his hands and eyes to heaven, in mute thanksgiving for some moments.

'To-morrow,' I heard him say; 'the commissioner will be here, and the Inquisition will be held according to law.'

Then turning to the old man with the gold spectacles, whom I have described, he shook him warmly by both hands and said:

'Baron, how can I thank you? How can we all thank you? You will have delivered this region from a plague that has scourged its inhabitants for more than a century. The horrible enemy, thank God, is at last tracked.'

My father led the stranger aside, and the General followed. I knew that he had led them out of hearing, that he might relate my case, and I saw them glance often quickly at me, as the discussion proceeded.

My father came to me, kissed me again and again, and leading me from the chapel, said:

'It is time to return, but before we go home, we must add to our party the good priest, who lives but a little way from this; and persuade him to accompany us to the schloss.'

In this quest we were successful: and I was glad, being unspeakably fatigued when we reached home. But my satisfaction was changed to dismay, on discovering that there were no tidings of Carmilla. Of the scene that had occurred in the ruined chapel, no explanation was offered to me, and it was clear that it was a secret which my father for the present determined to keep from me.

The sinister absence of Carmilla made the remembrance of the scene more horrible to me. The arrangements for that night were singular. Two servants, and Madame were to sit up in my room that night; and the ecclesiastic with my father kept watch in the adjoining dressing-room.

The priest had performed certain solemn rites that night, the purport of which I did not understand any more than I comprehended the reason of this extraordinary precaution taken for my safety during sleep.

I saw all clearly a few days later.

The disappearance of Carmilla was followed by the discontinuance of my nightly sufferings.

You have heard, no doubt, of the appalling superstition that prevails in Upper and Lower Styria, in Moravia, Silisia,[3] in Turkish Servia,[4] in Poland, even in Russia; the superstition, so we must call it, of the Vampire.

If human testimony, taken with every care and solemnity, judicially, before commissions innumerable, each consisting of many members, all chosen for integrity and intelligence, and constituting reports more voluminous perhaps than exist upon any one other class of cases, is worth anything, it is difficult to deny, or even to doubt the existence of such a phenomenon as the Vampire.

For my part I have heard no theory by which to explain what I myself have witnessed and experienced, other than that supplied by the ancient and well-attested belief of the country.

The next day the formal proceedings took place in the Chapel of Karnstein. The grave of the Countess Mircalla was opened; and the General and my father recognised each his perfidious and beautiful guest, in the face now disclosed to view. The features, though a hundred and fifty years had passed since her funeral, were tinted with the warmth of life. Her eyes were open; no cadaverous smell exhaled from the coffin. The two medical men, one officially present, the other on the part of the promoter of the inquiry, attested the marvellous fact, that there was a faint but appreciable respiration, and a corresponding action of the heart. The limbs were perfectly flexible, the flesh elastic; and the leaden coffin floated with blood, in which to a depth of seven inches, the body lay immersed. Here then, were all the admitted signs and proofs of vampirism. The body, therefore, in accordance with the ancient practice, was raised, and a sharp stake driven through the heart of the vampire, who uttered a piercing shriek at the moment, in all respects such as might escape from a living person in the last agony. Then the head was struck off, and a torrent of blood flowed from the severed neck. The body and head were next placed on a pile of wood, and reduced to ashes, which were thrown upon the river and borne away, and that territory has never since been plagued by the visits of a vampire.

My father has a copy of the report of the Imperial Commission, with the signatures of all who were present at these proceedings, attached in verification of the statement. It is from this official paper that I have summarized my account of this last shocking scene.

CHAPTER XVI.

Conclusion.

I write all this you suppose with composure. But far from it; I cannot think of it without agitation. Nothing but your earnest desire so repeatedly expressed, could have induced me to sit down to a task that has unstrung my nerves for months to come, and reinduced a shadow of the unspeakable horror which years after my deliverance continued to make my days and nights dreadful, and solitude insupportably terrific.[1]

Let me add a word or two about that quaint Baron Vordenburg, to whose curious lore we were indebted for the discovery of the Countess Mircalla's grave.

He had taken up his abode in Gratz, where, living upon a mere pittance, which was all that remained to him of the once princely estates of his family, in Upper Styria, he devoted himself to the minute and laborious investigation of the marvellously authenticated tradition of Vampirism. He had at his fingers' ends all the great and little works upon the subject. 'Magia Posthuma,' 'Phlegon de Mirabilibus,' 'Augustinus de curâ pro Mortuis,' 'Philosophicæ et Christianæ Cogitationes de Vampiris,' by John Christofer Herenberg;[2] and a thousand others, among which I remember only a few of those which he lent to my father. He had a voluminous digest of all the judicial cases, from which he had extracted a system of principles that appear to govern—some always, and others occasionally only—the condition of the vampire. I may mention, in passing, that the deadly pallor attributed to that sort of *revenants*, is a mere melodramatic fiction. They present, in the grave, and when they show themselves in human society, the appearance of healthy life. When disclosed to light in their coffins, they exhibit all the symptoms that are enumerated as those which proved the vampire-life of the long-dead Countess Karnstein.

How they escape from their graves and return to them for certain hours every day, without displacing the clay or leaving any trace of disturbance in the state of the coffin or the cerements, has always been admitted to be utterly inexplicable. The amphibious existence of the vampire is sustained by daily renewed slumber in the grave. Its horrible lust for living blood supplies the vigour of its waking existence. The vampire is prone to be fascinated with an engrossing vehemence, resembling the passion of love, by particular persons. In pursuit of these it will exercise inexhaustible patience and stratagem, for access to a particular object may be obstructed in a hundred ways. It will never desist until it has satiated its passion, and drained the very life of its coveted victim. But it will, in these cases, husband and protract its murderous enjoyment with the refinement of an epicure, and heighten it by the gradual approaches of an artful courtship. In these cases it seems to yearn for something like sympathy and consent. In ordinary ones it goes direct to its object, overpowers with violence, and strangles and exhausts often at a single feast.

The vampire is, apparently, subject, in certain situations, to special conditions. In the particular instance of which I have given you a relation, Mircalla seemed to be limited to a name which, if not her real one, should at least reproduce, without the omission or addition of a single letter, those, as we say, anagrammatically, which compose it. *Carmilla* did this; so did *Millarca*.

My father related to the Baron Vordenburg, who remained with us for two or three weeks after the expulsion of Carmilla, the story about the Moravian nobleman and the vampire at Karnstein churchyard, and then he asked the Baron how he had discovered the exact position of the long-concealed tomb of the Countess Mircalla? The Baron's grotesque features puckered up into a mysterious smile; he looked down, still smiling on his worn spectacle-case, and fumbled with it. Then looking up, he said:

'I have many journals, and other papers, written by that remarkable man; the most curious among them is one treating of the visit of which you speak, to Karnstein. The tradition, of course, discolours and distorts a little. He might have been termed a Moravian nobleman, for he had changed his abode to that territory, and was, beside, a noble. But he was, in truth, a native of Upper Styria. It is enough to say that in very early youth he had been a passionate and favored lover of the beautiful Mircalla, Countess Karnstein. Her early death plunged him into inconsolable grief. It is the nature of vampires to increase and multiply, but according to an ascertained[3] and ghostly law.

'Assume, at starting, a territory perfectly free from that pest. How does it begin, and how does it multiply itself? I will tell you. A person, more or less wicked, puts an end to himself. A suicide, under certain circumstances, becomes a vampire. That spectre visits living people in their slumbers; *they* die, and almost invariably, in the grave, develope[4] into vampires. This happened in the case of the beautiful Mircalla, who was haunted by one of those demons. My ancestor, Vordenburg, whose title I still bear, soon discovered this, and in the course of the studies to which he devoted himself, learned a great deal more.

'Among other things, he concluded that suspicion of vampirism would probably fall, sooner or later, upon the dead Countess, who in life had been his idol. He conceived a horror, be she what she might, of her remains being profaned by the outrage of a posthumous execution. He has left a curious paper to prove that the vampire, on its expulsion from its amphibious existence, is projected into a far more horrible life; and he resolved to save his once beloved Mircalla from this.

'He adopted the stratagem of a journey here, a pretended removal of her remains, and a real obliteration of her monument. When age had stolen upon him, and from the vale of years he looked back on the scenes he was leaving, he considered, in a different spirit, what he had done, and a horror took possession of him. He made the tracings and notes which have guided me to the very spot, and drew up a confession of the deception that he had practised. If he had intended any further action in this matter, death prevented him; and the hand of a remote descendant has, too late for many, directed the pursuit to the lair of the beast.'

We talked a little more, and among other things he said was this:

'One sign of the vampire is the power of the hand. The slender hand of Mircalla closed like a vice of steel on the General's wrist when he raised the hatchet to strike. But its power is not confined to its grasp; it leaves a numbness in the limb it seizes, which is slowly, if ever, recovered from.'

The following Spring my father took me a tour[5] through Italy. We remained away for more than a year. It was long before the terror of recent events subsided; and to this hour the image of

Carmilla returns to memory with ambiguous alternations—sometimes the playful, languid, beautiful girl; sometimes the writhing fiend I saw in the ruined church; and often from a reverie I have started, fancying I heard the light step of Carmilla at the drawing-room door.

Acknowledgements

I am grateful to Elda Rotor and Elizabeth Vogt of Penguin Classics for initiating and guiding this project with care and patience, and to Xiao Windy Xue for her generous and efficient assistance in preparing texts. I would also like to thank Karen Winstead for first proposing this volume, William Hughes for his unwavering support, and, as always, Joanne Parker and my family. This edition is dedicated to Paul, Fi, and Amy Reddaway—thank you.

INTRODUCTION

1. Peter J. Bräunlein, 'The Frightening Borderlands of Enlighten-ment: The Vampire Problem', *Studies in History and Philosophy of Biological and Biomedical Sciences* 43 (2012): 710–19, at 715.
2. 'Caleb D'Anvers' [Nicholas Amhurst], *The Craftsman*, 14 vols, no. 307 (Saturday, 20 May 1732); IX:120–29, at 127.
3. 'Lord Byron' [William Hone], *Don Juan: with A Biographical Account of Lord Byron and his Family; Anecdotes of his Lord-ship's Travels and Residence in Greece, at Geneva, &c. Includ-ing, also, A Sketch of the Vampyre Family . . . Canto III* (William Wright, 1819), pp. 67–8.
4. [Henry Southern,] 'Personal Character of Lord Byron', *The Lon-don Magazine* 10 (October 1824): 337–47, at 338, 341.
5. *Oxford English Dictionary*.
6. For a full discussion, see Nick Groom, '*The Vampyre*, Aubrey, and *Frankenstein*', in Sam George and Bill Hughes (eds.), *The Legacy of John Polidori: The Romantic Vampire and its Prog-eny* (Manchester University Press, 2024), pp. 123–40.
7. [Anon.,] 'Fictitious History of the Vampyre', *The Imperial Magazine; or, Compendium of Religious, Moral, & Philosoph-ical Knowledge* 1.3 (1819), cols 236–9, at col. 236.
8. John Coleman, *Fifty Years of an Actor's Life*, 2 vols (Hutchin-son & Co., 1904); I:30.
9. 'On Vampires and Vampirism', *The New Monthly Magazine* 14, pt. 2 (1820): 548–52, at 548.

10. *Monthly Review* 89 (May–August 1819): 87–96, at 90.
11. See Nick Groom, 'Thomas Chatterton and the Death of John William Polidori: Copycat or Coincidence?', *Notes & Queries* 67.4 (2020): 534–6.
12. Martin Willis, 'Le Fanu's "Carmilla", Ireland, and Diseased Vision', in Sharon Ruston (ed.), *Literature and Science* (Boydell & Brewer, 2008), pp. 111–130, at p. 111; see also Victor Sage, *Le Fanu's Gothic: The Rhetoric of Darkness* (Palgrave, 2004), pp. 178–201.
13. Matthew Gibson, *Dracula and the Eastern Question: British and French Vampire Narratives of the Nineteenth-Century Near East* (Palgrave Macmillan, 2006), p. 42; see also pp. 44–68.
14. R. F. Foster, *Words Alone: Yeats & his Inheritances* (Oxford University Press, 2011), p. 102.
15. See Nick Groom (ed.), *Romantic and Victorian Vampire Tales* (Oxford University Press, 2026).

The Vampyre

BY JOHN POLIDORI

1819 INTRODUCTION BY ALARIC WATTS

1. The Great Schism of 1054, which separated the Western Catholic Church (Latin) from the Eastern Orthodox Church (Greek).
2. Arnold Paul (the name is variously spelt) was a guerilla soldier and alleged vampire; in 1731, his case was thoroughly investigated by medical officers of the imperial Habsburg army, the report of which was published across Europe in 1732.
3. Corpses.
4. George Gordon, Lord Byron's 'Fragment of a Turkish Tale': his poem *The Giaour* (1813), ll. 757–88, with minor variations from the published text.
5. Robert Southey's Islamic epic *Thalaba the Destroyer*, 2 vols (1801).
6. Asserts, contends.

7. Joseph Pitton de Tournefort, *A Voyage into the Levant* (1718), which includes a report from 1701 of a 'Vroucolacas' on the Aegean island of Mykonos, and Dom Augustin Calmet's 1746 *Dissertations upon the Apparitions of Angels, Dæmons, and Ghosts, and concerning the Vampires of Hungary, Bohemia, Moravia, and Silesia* (published in English in 1759), which was effectively the standard handbook of northern European vampirology for a century.

THE VAMPYRE

1. Chic society.
2. Mental lethargy resulting from listlessness.
3. An allusion to Byron's lover Lady Caroline Lamb, who included their affair in her novel *Glenarvon* (1816); the account scandalized the reading public and wrecked Lamb's reputation.
4. A street entertainer, often associated with selling quack cures; Lamb had cross-dressed as a serving boy in her affair with Byron.
5. In the early part of the tale Aubrey has some affinity with Polidori himself.
6. Alluding to the cult of the picturesque, which encouraged artists to romanticize their subjects.
7. In short.
8. Fashionable, but with undertones of ostentation, vulgarity, and debauchery.
9. Accumulation.
10. The name is taken from Lamb's novel, Lord Glenarvon being Clarence Ruthven (pronounced *riven*).
11. Anna Laetitia Barbauld, 'Hymn XXIII: Praise to the Creator', l. 28 (1772).
12. An often rowdy card game illegal in Britain.
13. Guilder, coinage of the Netherlands.
14. Polidori had travelled across Europe in Byron's Napoleonic carriage.
15. Byron's poem *The Giaour* outlines the belief that Muslim men would be rewarded in paradise with beautiful houris with gazelle-like eyes.

16. The name, literally 'violet flower', alludes to the sea nymphs of Greek mythology.
17. Again referring to Byron's *The Giaour*, 'blue-winged butterfly of Kashmeer' (p. 8n.); probably the Adonis Blue.
18. Second-century Greek geographer.
19. Intemperate feasting.
20. The Saronic Gulf of the Aegean Sea.
21. Lane or gorge.
22. A banker's order for the withdrawal of money.
23. *Sic*; stunned, an obsolete meaning.
24. Ancient Greek city and port in Anatolia on the Aegean coast, now İzmir in Turkey.
25. Most easterly coastal town in Italy; possibly alluding to *The Castle of Otranto* (1764), Horace Walpole's early Gothic novel.
26. Long dagger usually sheathed in silver.
27. Childlike.
28. Sybarite or sensualist.
29. Society event for the presentation of débutantes—the first public appearance of a young lady of the upper class.
30. High society.
31. Take sustenance.
32. Satan, in the appearance of a persuasive snake, beguiled Eve in the Garden of Eden: see Genesis chapter 3 and John Milton's *Paradise Lost* (1667) book 9.
33. Entreating, imploring.

Carmilla

BY SHERIDAN LE FANU

PROLOGUE

1. An invented quotation suggesting life and the afterlife (or death), as well as dualities such as male and female.

CHAPTER I: An Early Fright

1. A region associated with vampire activity in the eighteenth century that today covers south-east Austria and north-east Slovenia.
2. An official of the Habsburg Empire.
3. City in Switzerland, the effective capital.
4. Hubbub of voices, alluding to the biblical Tower of Babel.
5. Governesses.
6. The phantasmagoria was an early moving-image spectacle achieved using magic lantern slides (see chapter IV, note 4).

CHAPTER II: A Guest

1. Temperate.
2. The 'Od' force was believed to be an emanation from sensitive people or particular objects that produced mesmeric effects.
3. Shakespeare, *The Merchant of Venice*, 1.1.1–3.
4. Sudden lurch of bolting horses.
5. Leather straps harnessing a horse to a carriage.

CHAPTER III: We Compare Notes

1. Generic name for a cat.
2. Cleopatra was popularly believed to have committed suicide by allowing herself to be bitten by venomous Egyptian cobras.

CHAPTER IV: Her Habits—A Saunter

1. Heraldic coat of arms.
2. Incoherent sounds.
3. Shivering.
4. An optical projector of images used to create uncanny or comic visual effects in phantasmagoria shows.
5. A herb accorded magical properties and reputed to scream when taken from the ground.
6. Fencing swords and face guards.

7. Protection.
8. Vampire (French).
9. French naturalist the Comte de Buffon (1707–88).
10. A mythical hybrid of eagle and horse.

CHAPTER V: A Wonderful Likeness

1. Capital of Styria.
2. Likeness (archaic).
3. Fantasy, but the word was beginning to gain meanings of love and passion.

CHAPTER VI: A Very Strange Agony

1. Literally drinking tea from the saucer, so as to cool it.
2. Travelling rapidly by changing horses.

CHAPTER VII: Descending

1. Both names change in the text.
2. *Sic.*
3. A Neapolitan lake believed to be an entrance to the underworld.
4. Broken up.
5. To a contemporary, Laura's appearance is that of a serial masturbator.

CHAPTER VIII: Search

1. Cupboard.
2. Steward and subordinates.
3. Treatments for sleeplessness and loss of consciousness.

CHAPTER IX: The Doctor

1. A bruise, characteristic of vampire attacks in the eighteenth century.
2. Travel bags.

CHAPTER X: Bereaved

1. Actively promote.

CHAPTER XI: The Story

1. Supernatural aid, alluding to the story of Aladdin in *The Arabian Nights' Entertainments*; Aladdin possessed a magic lamp that housed a jinn or genie, able to grant wishes and bring him extravagant wealth.
2. *Sic.*

CHAPTER XII: A Petition

1. Lengthy.

CHAPTER XIII: The Wood-Man

1. Nightmares—personified as the 'incubus', bearing down on the chest, and smothering the victim—were characteristic of eighteenth-century vampire reports.
2. One who returns from the dead, often seeking vengeance.
3. Those suspected of being vampires were exhumed to determine whether their corpses remained fresh, which was considered sufficient proof; their coffins were often also described as being awash with blood.
4. Today part of the Czech Republic.

CHAPTER XIV: The Meeting

1. Woeful.
2. Base.

CHAPTER XV: Ordeal and Execution

1. Brim.
2. Coat of arms.

3. Silesia.
4. Serbia.

CHAPTER XVI: Conclusion

1. Terrifying.
2. Standard eighteenth-century works of vampirology and the undead.
3. Certain (archaic).
4. Contemporary variant of 'develop'.
5. *Sic.*

EDITIONS

Joseph Sheridan Le Fanu, *Carmilla: A Critical Edition*, ed. Kathleen Costello-Sullivan (Syracuse University Press, 2013).

Sheridan Le Fanu, *In a Glass Darkly*, ed. Robert Tracy (Oxford University Press, 2008).

John William Polidori, *The Diary of Dr. John William Polidori, 1816: Relating to Byron, Shelley, etc.*, ed. William Michael Rossetti (Elkin Mathews, 1911).

John William Polidori, *The Vampyre and Ernestus Berchtold; or, The Modern Oedipus: Collected Fiction of John William Polidori*, ed. D. L. Macdonald and Kathleen Scherf (University of Toronto Press, 1994).

John William Polidori, *The Vampyre and Ernestus Berchtold; or, The Modern Œdipus*, ed. D. L. Macdonald and Kathleen Scherf (Broadview Press, 2007).

John William Polidori, *The Vampyre and Other Tales of the Macabre*, ed. Robert Morrison and Chris Baldick (Oxford University Press, 1998; 2nd edn, 2008).

Mary Shelley, *Frankenstein or The Modern Prometheus. The 1818 Text*, ed. Nick Groom (Oxford University Press, 2019).

Bram Stoker, *Dracula*, ed. Roger Luckhurst (Oxford University Press, 2011).

GENERAL STUDIES

Richard Adelman, 'Ruskin & Gothic Literature', *The Wordsworth Circle* 48.3 (2017): pp. 152–64.

Simon Bacon (ed.), *The Palgrave Handbook of the Vampire* (Palgrave Macmillan [Springer Nature, Switzerland], 2024).

Paul Barber, *Vampires, Burial, and Death: Folklore and Reality*, 2nd edn (Yale University Press, 2010).

Harry Benshoff, 'The Monster and the Homosexual', in Jeffrey Andrew Weinstock (ed.), *The Monster Theory Reader* (University of Minnesota Press, 2020), pp. 226–40.

Naomi Booth, 'Vampiric Swoons and Other Dark Ecologies', in *Swoon: A Poetics of Passing Out* (Manchester University Press, 2021), pp. 157–89.

Leo Braudy, *Haunted: On Ghosts, Witches, Vampires, Zombies, and Other Monsters of the Natural and Supernatural Worlds* (Yale University Press, 2016).

Peter J. Bräunlein, 'The Frightening Borderlands of Enlightenment: The Vampire Problem', *Studies in History and Philosophy of Biological and Biomedical Sciences* 43 (2012): pp. 710–19.

Elisabeth Bronfen, *Over Her Dead Body: Death, Femininity and the Aesthetic* (Manchester University Press, 1992).

Erik Butler, *Metamorphoses of the Vampire in Literature and Film: Cultural Transformations in Europe, 1732–1933* (Camden House, 2010).

Jeffrey Jerome Cohen (ed.), *Monster Theory: Reading Culture* (University of Minnesota Press, 1996).

Heide Crawford, *The Origins of the Literary Vampire* (Rowman & Littlefield, 2016).

Richard Davenport-Hines, *Gothic: 400 Years of Excess, Horror, Evil and Ruin* (Fourth Estate, 1998).

Peter Day (ed.), *Vampires: Myths and Metaphors of Enduring Evil* (Rodopi, 2006).

Alan Dundes (ed.), *The Vampire: A Casebook* (University of Wisconsin Press, 1998).

Jeffrey Freedman (ed.), *A Cultural History of Death*, Vol. IV: *A Cultural History of Death in the Age of Enlightenment* (Bloomsbury, 2024).

Ken Gelder, *Reading the Vampire* (Routledge, 1994).

Nick Groom, *The Vampire: A New History*, 2nd edn (Yale University Press, 2020).
Nick Groom and William Hughes (eds.), *The Vampire: An Edinburgh Companion* (Edinburgh University Press, 2025).
Ardel Haefele-Thomas, *Queer Others in Victorian Gothic: Transgressing Monstrosity* (University of Wales Press, 2012).
Klaus Hamberger, *Mortuus Non Mordet: Dokumente zum Vampirismus 1689–1791* (Turia & Kant, 1992).
Marie Mulvey-Roberts, *Dangerous Bodies: Historicising the Gothic Corporeal* (Manchester University Press, 2016).
Jan Louis Perkowski, *Vampire Lore: From the Writings of Jan Louis Perkowski* (Slavica Publishers, 2006).
David Punter (ed.), *A New Companion to the Gothic* (Wiley Blackwell, 2015).
Aspasia Stephanou, *Reading Vampire Gothic Through Blood: Bloodlines* (Palgrave Macmillan, 2014).
Andrew McConnell Stott, *The Poet and the Vampyre: The Curse of Byron and the Birth of Literature's Greatest Monsters* (Pegasus Books, 2014).
Roxana Stuart, *Stage Blood: Vampires of the 19th-Century Stage* (Bowling Green State University Popular Press, 1994).
James Twitchell, *The Living Dead: A Study of the Vampire in Romantic Literature* (Duke University Press, 1981).

CRITICAL WORKS ON *THE VAMPYRE*

Simon Bainbridge, 'Lord Ruthven's Power: Polidori's "The Vampyre", Doubles and the Byronic Imagination', *The Byron Journal* 34.1 (2006): pp. 21–34.
Nick Groom, 'Polidori's "The Vampyre": Composition, Publication, Deception', *Romanticism* 28.1 (April 2022): pp. 46–59.
Nick Groom, '*The Vampyre*, Aubrey, and *Frankenstein*', in Sam George and Bill Hughes (eds.), *The Legacy of John Polidori: The Romantic Vampire and its Progeny* (Manchester University Press, 2024), pp. 123–40.
Diane Long Hoeveler, *The Gothic Ideology: Religious Hysteria and Anti-Catholicism in British Popular Fiction, 1780–1880* (University of Wales Press, 2014).

D. L. Macdonald, *Poor Polidori: A Critical Biography of the Author of The Vampyre* (University of Toronto Press, 1991).

Bridget Marshall, 'An Evil Game: Gothic Villains and Gaming Addictions', *Gothic Studies* 11.2 (2009): pp. 9–18.

Ivan Phillips, '"But if thine eye be evil": Tropes of Vision in the Rise of the Modern Vampire', in Sam George and Bill Hughes (eds.), *The Legacy of John Polidori*, pp. 167–85.

Patricia Skarda, 'Vampirism and Plagiarism: Byron's Influence and Polidori's Practice', *Studies in Romanticism* 28.2 (1989): pp. 249–69.

Anne Stiles, Stanley Finger, and John Bulevich, 'Somnambulism and Trance States in the Works of John William Polidori, Author of *The Vampyre*', *European Romantic Review* 21.6 (2010): 789–807.

Henry R. Viets, 'The London Editions of Polidori's "The Vampyre"', *Papers of the Bibliographical Society of America* 63.2 (1969): pp. 83–103.

CRITICAL WORKS ON *CARMILLA*

Gary William Crawford, Jim Rockhill, and Brian J. Showers (eds.), *Reflections in a Glass Darkly: Essays on J. Sheridan Le Fanu* (Hippocampus Press, 2011).

Maria Giakaniki, 'Wide Awake and Dreaming: The Night, the Haunt, and the Female Vampire', in Carol Margaret Davison (ed.), *Gothic Dreams and Nightmares* (Manchester University Press, 2024), pp. 149–66.

Stephanie Green, 'Time and the Vampire: The Idea of the Past in *Carmilla* and *Dracula*', in David Baker, Stephanie Green, and Agnieszka Stasiewicz-Bieńkowska (eds.), *Hospitality, Rape and Consent in Vampire Popular Culture* (Palgrave Macmillan, 2017), pp. 89–105.

W. J. McCormack and Valerie Wallace, *Sheridan Le Fanu and Victorian Ireland* (Lilliput Press, 1991).

Jarlath Killeen, *The Emergence of Irish Gothic Fiction: History, Origins, Theories* (Edinburgh University Press, 2013).

Diane Mason, '"The languor which I had long felt began to display itself in my countenance": Vampires, Lesbians and Masturbators', in *The Secret Vice: Masturbation in Victorian Fiction and Medical Culture* (Manchester University Press, 2008), pp. 50–74.

Amanda Paxton, 'Mothering by Other Means: Parasitism and J. Sheridan Le Fanu's *Carmilla*', *ISLE: Interdisciplinary Studies in Literature and Environment* 28.1 (2021): pp. 166–85.

Victor Sage, *Le Fanu's Gothic: The Rhetoric of Darkness* (London: Palgrave, 2004).

Julieann Ulin, 'Sheridan Le Fanu's Vampires and Ireland's Invited Invasion', in Sam George and Bill Hughes (eds.), *Open Graves, Open Minds: Representations of Vampires and the Undead from the Enlightenment to the Present Day* (Manchester University Press, 2013), pp. 39–55.

William Veeder, '"Carmilla": The Arts of Repression', in Fred Botting and Dale Townshend (eds.), *Gothic: Critical Concepts in Literary and Cultural Studies*, Vol. III: *Nineteenth-Century Gothic: At Home with the Vampire* (Routledge, 2004), pp. 117–41.

Martin Willis, 'Le Fanu's "Carmilla", Ireland, and Diseased Vision', in Sharon Ruston (ed.), *Literature and Science* (Boydell & Brewer, 2008), pp. 111–30.

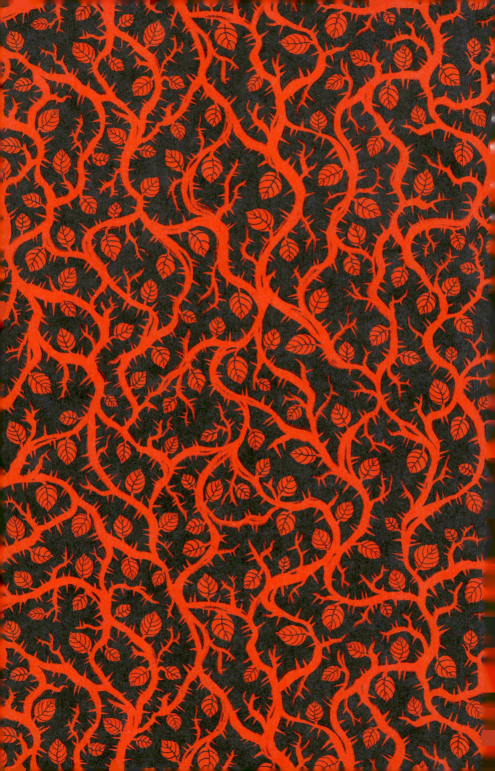